There was a shocked stillness in the air

Cringing with embarrassment, exposed as she was to him, Amber whispered, "Let me go, Dyson." She was past pleading, but her words came out huskily.

Bending his head, almost as if paying homage, Dyson kissed both of her breasts. "I want to touch you—to hold you," he said as if entranced. "I don't want to hurt your lovely body." He seemed to force his gaze from her breasts to her face, and Amber saw something there that told her he had a much greater sensitivity than ever she would have believed.

"Yet you are hurting me, aren't you," she murmured, "and I think you're hurting yourself, too, Dyson." Amber didn't know how she knew that, but at the moment she was certain of nothing else.

JESSICA STEELE
is also the author of these

Harlequin Presents

and these
Harlequin Romances

Many of these books are available at your local bookseller.

For a free catalog listing all titles currently available,
send your name and address to:

HARLEQUIN READER SERVICE
1440 South Priest Drive, Tempe, AZ 85281
Canadian address: Stratford, Ontario N5A 6W2

JESSICA STEELE

intimate enemies

Harlequin Books

TORONTO • NEW YORK • LOS ANGELES • LONDON
AMSTERDAM • PARIS • SYDNEY • HAMBURG
STOCKHOLM • ATHENS • TOKYO • MILAN

Harlequin Presents first edition June 1983
ISBN 0-373-10605-X

Original hardcover edition published in 1979
by Mills & Boon Limited

CHAPTER ONE

THE girl lying quietly in the narrow bed drifted slowly up from her drugged sleep. She was unsurprised to find a nurse bending over her. It had happened before —was it yesterday or the day previously? It didn't matter—nothing mattered any more.

'How are you feeling?'

'Fine,' she replied

It was becoming a stock answer. What did the sometimes excruciating pain in her back and the rest of her body matter, compared with the ache in her heart? Why couldn't she have been killed along with her beloved parents that last terrible day of their holiday in North Wales? They had had no warning that disaster was about to strike as they had scrambled up the rocky mountainside, her parents insisting they were still as fit and as strong as any youngster of the next generation. She could see her father laughing as he had made some crack as he had beaten her to the next point in their explorations, could see now his laughter change to sheer horror as a sound above them made them all look up to see the cascade of rocks bearing down on them. Her eyes widened in alarm as the remembrance hit her with haunting clarity.

'I'll get you something for the pain,' the nurse by her side told her gently, before scurrying off in search of Sister.

How long had she lain here? Amber had no idea, and didn't care very much either. She knew she wasn't making the progress expected of her, knew vaguely, though no one had told her, that she had been transferred from the hospital she had first been taken to to the hospital in Exeter in an attempt to get her to show some interest in the business of living. They had been mistaken in thinking that transferring her to where her friends could more easily visit her would buck her up. She wanted to be with her mum and dad—wanted to die too. Exeter was where she had been born and brought up, and she suspected Uncle James had had a hand in her being moved. Not that Uncle James was a proper uncle, but as well as being a doctor, he was a long-standing family friend.

The nurse returned with Sister in tow, and they went through the, 'How are you feeling?' and 'Fine,' routine again.

'I can't give you another injection until the doctor has seen you,' the Sister said gently. 'But he should be here soon—then you can have a nice sleep.'

Amber turned her pain-filled brown eyes in the Sister's direction. 'It doesn't matter,' she said softly.

Everyone was being so kind and patient with her, and she regretted that it was too much of an effort for her to try and get well again. But get well for what? Theirs had been such a close family unit—just her, her mother and father. They had gone everywhere together. She had plenty of acquaintances, but didn't have too many friends of her own age. It had been a family joke that at twenty-two she had shown no signs of wanting to leave the family nest. She could hear her father now, that twinkle in his voice as he had said, 'You've made it too comfortable for her, Susie—we'll never have the place to ourselves.' And her reply, 'And who would bring your early morning tea if I wasn't around? Not many families have a built-in chambermaid!' And her father looking faintly regretful before he had given her a hug that showed her that next to his wife he loved his daughter best in the whole world. 'In that case,' he had sighed, 'you'd better stay.'

Her thoughts were interrupted as the pain some-where at the base of her spine got worse—she tried to relax, tried to let it wash over her, but it wouldn't go away. Kept on insisting she should concentrate her thoughts on nothing other than where she was and if she didn't like the pain she should make some effort to get well and so be rid of its nagging.

When the visiting consultant entered the side ward she had been placed in, Amber was gritting her teeth against the intense pain, her hands gripping the side of the bed in an effort not to cry out.

Mr Phillips took one look at her and straight away ordered the Sister at his side to prepare an injection, then turning to Amber, 'Are you going to tell me too that you're feeling fine?' he asked, his severe, clever face showing a hint of a smile as he looked down at the pale girl in the bed, his voice booming in her ears.

'Would you believe me?' Amber replied wearily. If Sister didn't appear with that injection soon, she had an idea she would soon start screaming, for her back felt as if was about to break in two.

Then mercifully Sister was there, and a syringe was being emptied into her arm, and while Mr Phillips was still with her, asking her questions in that booming voice of his, questions she was sure he had asked a dozen times before, she felt the pain begin to leave her.

She had no idea how long Mr Phillips was with her. She was aware of his examination, but felt little pain as his gentle fingers probed over the stitched and lacerated lower back. Then a nurse in assistance was replacing the covers and saying, 'Does that feel com-fortable?'

'Yes, thank you,' Amber muttered, her eyelids already beginning to droop. She would sleep soon, she knew, but she opened her eyes as the trio disappeared from her vision and enclosed her once more behind the screens.

She couldn't for the moment figure out why the screens were there at all. They hadn't been there yesterday, and she knew she was the only patient in the side ward. Drowsily she thought perhaps it was one of Mr Phillips' quirks that he insisted on screens wherever he went. Uncle James had told her on one of his visits that Mr Phillips was the best man in his field, so no wonder his little peculiarities were observed without question. Amber closed her eyes again.

'She's in very bad shape,' she heard Mr Phillips' voice float over the screens, and knew he was talking about her. Then Sister added something, though her voice was much quieter.

The next thing Mr Phillips said had Amber's eyes coming wide open, sleep that had been so near hurtling away. 'Keep her in this side ward, Sister, though I'm very much afraid she's not going to be with us much longer—if she pulls through this she won't live longer than six months anyway.'

He had to be talking about her, she was the only person in the small side ward. And suddenly, as the consultant's words screamed through her brain, Amber knew that far from wanting to die as she had thought not many minutes earlier, she wanted to live. Oh no, he can't mean me, she thought, as his death sentence of six months echoed and re-echoed in her brain fighting against the effects of the injection she had been given. I want to live.

The medication had had its effect when Mr Phillips left the side ward, and Sister, taking a peep behind the screens, saw that Amber Newman, the girl they were all working so hard to get back on her feet, was sound asleep.

Amber awakened to find the screens no longer round

her. She remembered immediately the last words she had heard Mr Phillips say, and knew as she glanced round the small room, the only other bed there empty as it had always been, that he had been speaking about her. Panic such as she could never remember feeling before hit her, and for the first time since she had been brought to the hospital she put her fingers on the button and rang for the nurse. She didn't want to be on her own.

She was in tears when the nurse came hurrying in to see what she wanted, but Amber couldn't tell her what was troubling her. She was twenty-two and wanted to live. To say that out loud would have her hysterical, she thought.

'Is the pain very bad?' the nurse asked sympathetically, mopping at Amber's tears with a tissue from the box on her locker. 'We can't give you an injection yet, dear—it's too soon after your last one.'

'It isn't that,' Amber sobbed.

'What is it, then?' Nurse Jones asked soothingly. She took hold of Amber's hand, and Amber gripped it tightly. 'Come on, you can tell me,' she coaxed gently, and when Amber still couldn't tell her, 'It's your parents, isn't it?' she guessed, thinking the sobbing girl must be crying over her parents. Nurse Jones stayed with Amber for as long as she could, and over the next few weeks devoted all her experience and attention to getting Amber on her feet again.

For Amber those weeks were often painful. But the physical pain lessened, and though she began to suffer terrible nightmares, she began to adjust to the loss of her parents. But she could not adjust to the knowledge that she would be joining them before the next six months were out. She was stricken by panic every time the thought hit her, which was often, but she still could not confide in anyone that she had heard what Mr Phillips had said.

At the end of three weeks she was pronounced fit enough to go home. They're sending me home to die, she thought, and tried to be brave, but knew she wasn't brave at all, though she managed to keep her feelings from showing when Mr Phillips came to see her for the last time.

'You've made a good recovery,' he told her, and she let him think she believed him, her face expressionless as she listened to him. 'We've had quite a tussle with you, young lady, so don't go doing anything silly and undoing all our good work.'

'I won't,' Amber assured him, thinking since he couldn't bring himself to tell her the truth, she might as well play the game his way.

'You'll have to take things easy for at least six months,' he was telling her. Six months, she thought, and tried not to panic again that what he was really telling her was that six months was all she had. 'Your spine was badly bruised under that rock fall,' he went on, 'and you didn't help at all by trying to struggle out and get to your parents, but you've had blood pumped back into you, and except for the scars where you were stitched—which will hardly show in time—the scars from your other cuts will disappear completely.' He smiled at her as if he thought vanity was the only worry she had on her mind at that moment.

'Thank you,' Amber said, because she didn't know what else she was expected to say.

'The best way you can thank me is by following my advice. Don't go doing anything silly. No lifting or carrying. Not too much standing,' another smile. 'Treat your body gently for six months,' he said.

Amber thanked him again, and before she left the hospital she went and thanked personally all the nursing staff who had looked after her, and in particular Carol Jones. James Cresswell collected her and took her back to the semi-detached she had last seen the day she had left to go on holiday with her parents.

'Here we are. Amber—I don't like you being on your own. Are you sure you won't come and stay with me? There's plenty of room and you know Mrs Paget would love to have someone to fuss over.' He looked fondly at the lovely young girl who was as dear to him as a daughter.

'No, Uncle James. I appreciate your offer, I really do,' Amber told him with a smile, 'but—but I've got to adjust some time to living without Mum and Dad—I'd rather start now.' Even to Uncle James, she couldn't reveal what he must as her G.P. also know; the hospital was bound to have put him in the picture. She secretly thought Mrs Paget, his housekeeper, had enough to do in looking after a doctor's house, taking the innumerable phone calls, besides her other duties, without having a convalescent on her hands.

James Cresswell insisted on carrying her case up to her room. 'No lifting,' he reminded her, when she said she could take it up herself. He stayed and had a cup of coffee with her, and suddenly she didn't want to be on her own. She bottled down the growing feeling of disquiet, knowing how busy Uncle James' practice kept him, and the unfairness of keeping him with her for company.

'I'll give you a prescription for some more painkillers,' he said before he got up to go. 'Those that the hospital gave you won't last very long—remember now,' he joked, 'no drinking or driving while you're taking them!'

Amber smiled back at him because it was what he expected of her; she didn't drive and seldom drank. She wondered if she would be taking pain-killers up to the day it was all over, for though Mr Phillips had told her her back was healing, it was not doing so without letting her know about it.

'I won't,' she promised.

'I'll be popping in from time to time, but come and see me at the surgery if you're anxious about anything.'

She saw the professional look he flicked over her, and forced a smile. 'I'll be fine now,' she said.

But she wasn't fine. She tried to stick it out on her own, but added to the disquiet of her thoughts, was the emptiness of the house without her parents in it. She had gone into their room the day she came home and the alarm of her feelings had been buried in the grief that had swamped her, and she had just sat on the bed where she had greeted them every morning with their tea, and had cried until she could cry no more.

A week after she had been discharged from hospital she knew that if she didn't do something about the alternating panic and depression that lived with her, she would end up at the funny farm before the six months were up. In sheer desperation she came to terms with herself. She was twenty-two, a quite normal girl of average intelligence, she thought. She was well thought of in her job with the firm of solicitors where she worked as a secretary, but knew from the way she had to keep taking pain-killers that a day spent sitting at her typewriter would have her flat on her back for a week—even if Uncle James allowed her to go back to work, which she knew he wouldn't. But where was she? Who was she? Cocooned as she had been in the love of her parents, the loving family unit, she knew nothing of the outside world. She had occasional boy-friends, but nothing about them had stirred her to want to go overboard for them. But she couldn't go on like this—twenty-two, for God's sake, and in six months she would be dead. Terror rushed in again. Dead, and she hadn't yet begun to live. She controlled her panic, fought for something to take her mind from it. Was she going to take it lying down? Had she no more backbone than to sit at home waiting for it?

She got to her feet, ready to fight against fate. She wasn't sure what she was going to do, but was suddenly sure she wasn't going to give in. She was going to cram as much living as she could into the next six months. She grabbed up her coat and hurried out of the house. She had no idea where she was going to start, but one thing was certain, she didn't intend to sit at home and wait for death to call her.

The bus dropped her off near to the centre of Exeter, and today instead of making for the cathedral as she had yesterday, she turned her feet in the direction of a coffee house where a good few of her acquaintances congregated. The feeling of peace that had come to her once inside the cathedral hadn't lasted once she was outside, so she would try to find peace from her thoughts with some of the others in her age group.

But after two cups of coffee and seeing none of the people she knew—silly to think she would anyway, they would all be at work at this time of the day— Amber was just about to leave when a girl she did know came in.

Sally Smith saw her straight away, looked round as Amber had done to see if there was anyone else she knew there, and seeing no one she knew except Amber, came and took the seat opposite her.

'Not working?' Sally asked, looking round for someone to take her order.

'I'm off sick at the moment.'

'Oh yes, sorry, I'd forgotten—Linda Archer told me she'd been to see you in hospital. Are you better?'

'Yes, thanks,' Amber replied, and not wanting to talk about herself, asked Sally if she was working.

'Between jobs at the moment.'

'Boring, isn't it?' Amber opined.

'Depends what you do with your spare time,' Sally came back. 'Can't say I'm ever bored, there's always something doing somewhere.' She broke off to order her coffee, and since her cup was empty and at least Sally was someone to talk to, Amber ordered another cup she didn't want. 'There's plenty of life around here,' Sally went on, then gave a knowing smile. 'If you know where to look for it.'

Sally Smith wasn't a particularly close friend of Amber's, but since she seemed to know where the living was done, Amber's interest was caught. Sally seemed to stroll through life without a care, why couldn't she be the same? Even now, jobless, Sally didn't appear to have a care in the world, and Amber knew, since recalling that Sally lived in a flat by herself, that the rent would have to be found from somewhere.

'Where does—er—one look for all this life?' she asked, and caught Sally's speculative glance on her.

'Thinking of branching out?' she asked in turn, lifting one well plucked eyebrow.

'I'm in a bit of a rut at the moment,' Amber told her, eager now for anything Sally could enlighten her with.

'What's one of those?' Sally asked with the air of one who wouldn't know a rut if she saw one, and when Amber didn't answer her, but sat looking as though questioning her statement that she knew where it was all happening, Sally said, 'I haven't got anything arranged for tonight—come into town about eight if you like—we'll go on a pub crawl.'

Amber had never been on a pub crawl in her life, but as she started to get ready that night to meet Sally in the hotel she had named, she thought anything was better than staying at home waiting for the months to creep by.

It was a new experience for her to enter a hotel bar on her own. The bar was filling up already, but as yet Sally hadn't arrived. Amber saw the barman looking at her, knew she had too much lipstick on—in fact, in an attempt not to let Sally down she had been quite liberal with her make-up. The bartender looked at her questioningly, so lifting her head an inch or two higher she went up to the bar, and intent on proving to him she wasn't out of her element, ordered a whisky.

'With water?' he queried.

'No—just as it is,' she said, and wondered what she did now until Sally came. She looked round for a seat and spotted a bar stool empty some yards down. The stool didn't have a back to it, and she needed the support a chair would have given her, but what did it matter, she had taken her pain-killers before she had come out—she could take some more when she got home if her back started to protest at her lack of consideration.

She approached the stool, saw there was another one vacant next to it; good, that would do for Sally when she came. The operation of clambering up on to a bar stool was new to her, and she winced as she didn't make it the first time and slipped until her feet touched the floor.

'Want some help?' asked a deep-noted voice above her ear, and she looked up, blinking, felt herself being docketed as the 'eye-batting variety' as without further ado the tall dark-haired man stepped off his stool, gripped her round her waist and effortlessly lifted her on to the stool.

'Thank you,' she muttered, not at all happy at the way her knees were showing, but too momentarily in pain from the sudden movement to want to do anything about it.

Her whisky arrived, and the man who had sat her on her stool returned his attention to his drink in front of him. Amber tried an experimental sip of her whisky, didn't think too much of it, but since she had had worse-tasting medicine in hospital thought she would be able to finish it.

Where was Sally? She wished she would hurry up and get here. She flicked her eyes about, feeling as if everyone was looking at her, and quickly turned her eyes back to her glass as she saw the bartender give her what she could only describe as a knowing look. In two minds now about forgetting all about the planned pub crawl, the feeling of panic that was now quite familiar to her stormed through her, and she looked at the man on the next stool to hers, wanting someone to talk to—it didn't matter who, anyone would have done to get her over these few unbearable moments.

She saw he was looking morosely into his glass, his face stern. She didn't know what he'd got to be so glum about—and didn't particularly care. He wasn't going to die before six months were out, was he, his worries were nothing compared ... Gulping down the feeling that she wanted to scream and rail against fate at the top of her voice, she broke into brittle chatter, anything to keep her thoughts at bay.

'Cheer up,' she said, and when he turned his head to stare at her as though she'd just appeared from another planet. 'It can't be as bad as all that, surely?' She thought he was going to turn his attention back to contemplating his drink—he looked ready to ignore her. 'The sun will still be shining for you tomorrow,' she added quickly, forcing a smile that cost her dear, as she pushed the thought away that there wouldn't be too many sunshiny mornings left for her.

The man gave her a long, level look. 'You reckon?' he queried.

'Always does.' She was glad he hadn't ignored her. If only she could keep a conversation going with him until Sally got here! Anything was better than her own thoughts. 'I haven't seen you here before, have I?' she asked. She had never been here before, but he wasn't to know that.

He ignored her question and looked down at her glass. 'Want another?' he asked, and flicked his eyes over her too made-up face, his look derogatory.

Amber felt a different sort of panic as she realised he thought she had been angling for him to buy her a drink—thought she was trying to pick him up. 'Not at the moment.' She turned her face away from him so he shouldn't see how sick she was feeling with herself. Then an anger welled up inside her that he should judge her so without knowing her, before fairness ousted her anger and she faced squarely, what else should he have thought? She was propped up on a bar stool and on her own. True, he had made the first overtures when he had lifted her on to her seat, but from then on he had ignored her, and it had been she who had tried to strike up a conversation with him. He was back to staring in front of him again, her refusal to allow him to buy her a drink affecting him neither one way or the other. Amber twisted her body to get a look at the door to see if there was any sign of Sally coming in. Her action caused her to feel a twinge of pain in her back, and unwanted thoughts threatened to come screaming in again.

'Perhaps you'd like to buy me that drink later?' she heard herself saying, shock hitting her, drowning her panic, that in order to get someone to speak to her, take her mind off the thoughts she was desperate to get rid of, she could act this way. Her words had the effect of making the man turn his head in her direction, even if it was only to give her that derogatory look again.

'Perhaps I might,' he agreed. Then, his face perceptive, 'How old are you?'

'Over the age of consent,' Amber replied, thinking what did it matter anyway. She had wanted new experiences, hadn't she? Though this man looked as though there was nothing new for him to experience.

'By the look of you, you consent too readily,' he said brusquely, and turned his head away, a fact for which she was glad, because she didn't want him to see the mortifying blush that coloured her cheeks as the implication behind his words hit her.

'No one's ever complained about that before.' Oh no, what was she saying?—she had an idea this brittle surface chat had been getting too deep before. Any minute now he would say something and she wouldn't have a clue what he was talking about, and he'd be sure to see through her.

'I'm not complaining,' he said slowly. 'Girls like you have their uses.'

Already she wasn't sure of his meaning. She moved uncomfortably on her stool, the ache in her lower spine telling her she should have found a seat with a back rest to it.

'And you use girls like me often?' She hadn't intended saying anything more to him. He was outside her experience, but the niggle of pain was sufficient to bring the sick reminder of her limited future rushing in.

'I have never paid for—those sort of pleasures,' he said coolly.

'Who's asking you to?' Her face was aflame, she barely knew what was keeping her glued to her seat, then she recanted that thought. She did know. She needed someone to keep her mind off her thoughts, and though this conversation was sickening her to her stomach—for all there seemed to be little kindness in him for the rest of humanity—at least he was another human being.

'Are you offering yourself for free?' he asked bluntly.

'I'm not offering myself at all,' she said, and wished she hadn't, because now he would lose the infinitesimal interest in her that he had, and she would be left to let those unwanted panicky thoughts come accelerating in.

'Just out to tease?' he queried unexpectedly. 'You've picked on the wrong man, little girl.' He put his empty glass down on the bar top, and she suspected that any minute now, he would go.

'Don't go,' she said desperately, and thought something in her voice must have got through to him, for instead of getting up and walking away from her, he replaced his foot that had gone to the ground, back on the stool.

'Can you give me one good reason why I shouldn't?'

'Not really.' Amber looked into her glass. She couldn't tell anyone she knew why she needed company, she wasn't about to start with a complete stranger. 'I'm a bit fed up with myself at the moment. I ... I just—thought it might ...' her voice tailed off. She didn't look at him, but knew her plea for him to stay had gone unheeded. Then she was surprised into looking at him on hearing him say:

'I have problems enough of my own, so I can do without hearing yours—but since I'm fed up too ...' He looked down at her glass. 'Ready for that drink yet?'

'Not yet.' She smiled, glad he was staying. 'Do you live around here?' she asked, wanting to talk, but not knowing what one said in this peculiar situation she found herself in. She was suddenly sure Sally wasn't going to come now; she must have been sitting here for over half an hour.

'I live not too far away,' he said, not telling her where, and she realised then that whatever they spoke of until it was time for her to go, nothing of a personal nature must be allowed to enter their conversation. He wouldn't want to share confidences with the type of person he thought she was. She took another sip from her glass. Ships that pass on the night flipped through her mind, but where she was more a flimsy canoe, she thought he might well be a destroyer.

'You're not staying in this hotel, then?' she asked brightly when moments had passed with neither of them saying anything.

'As a matter of fact, for this evening I am.'

'Oh.' The small sound escaped her. Then her mind went on to what he had said about having enough problems of his own. He had said he lived not too far away —so why then was he staying in the hotel tonight? She could find no answer to that, and took another sip of her whisky, hiding the shudder that went through her as she had done before at a taste she didn't care for. Perhaps he's married, the thought suddenly struck her, and she flicked a hasty glance at his hands to see they were ringless, though that didn't signify anything very much. Perhaps he'd had a row with his wife? Her sense of decency threatened to overcome her need to have him with her, at that thought, before she considered; she wasn't doing any harm just sitting here talking to him.

'Your glass is almost empty—I've noticed you've been fidgeting about on that stool. How about having that drink I promised you in the comfort of my room?'

Amber knew then exactly what he was asking. If she went with him to his room, it could only end up one way. His reference to her fidgeting on her stool— he couldn't know it was because her back was playing up—brought back the reminder of things she was desperately trying to forget. Why shouldn't she go with him to his room? With or without her he would go soon, and she didn't want to be left on her own. She forced the fear of what she was letting herself in for from her mind, forced herself to remember she was twenty-two and hadn't lived yet, but uppermost in her mind was the thought that if she went with him she wouldn't be alone.

'Are you married?' she blurted out.

He looked momentarily surprised, as though he hadn't thought her the sort of girl to have scruples. 'No,' he said after studying her for a second or two. 'I'm not married.' He paused—the decision was all hers, she somehow knew he wouldn't press her.

'Perhaps your room would be more comfortable,' she found herself agreeing, and blanked off her mind as with his help she got down from her stool. She felt all eyes must be following her as she left the bar with him.

CHAPTER TWO

AMBER had cold feet long before the lift stopped at the floor that housed his room. What was she doing here? A picture of her parents flashed through her mind and she stood rooted to the spot as the lift doors opened and the man stepped outside waiting for her to join him.

'This way,' he said when she had forced herself to step outside the lift.

Silently she went with him, turning her thoughts away from the image that remembering her mother and father had evoked, away from the love that had bound the three of them, knowing there was no turning back. She wanted the warmth of a loving relationship, and swallowed nervously as the man opened the door to his room and indicated that she should go through. There would be no love passing between them, she knew that for a certainty, and she prayed he would be gentle with her—other girls did this sort of thing and thought nothing of it, only she never had. She found some comfort in the thought that this night at least she would not be spending the night tormented by nightmares in the solitary confines of her home. When she woke up she would have someone with her, she would not be alone.

She swallowed again on entering the room. It seemed to be dominated by the big double bed. She turned her head away from the bed, noticing there were two wooden-armed easy chairs in the room.

'I need to go to the bathroom,' she said in a rush.

'It sounds urgent,' her host replied easily. 'Through that door there.'

Her eyes followed the direction of the small incli-
nation of his head, and she left him, closing the bathroom door firmly behind her.

Not only was her back playing her up, but her head
was thundering too. She wondered briefly if that was
the effect of the whisky she had drunk, but didn't think
it was. She reached in her bag for her pain-killers, took
two although she wasn't due to take any for another
couple of hours. Then with a thought that her host
wouldn't be very pleased if she started complaining
with pain once the time came to share that bed with
him, she up-ended another couple of tablets into her
hand and hastily swallowed them with the reckless
thought, what did it matter anyway? Then as frightening thoughts began to take shape in her mind again,
the need for human contact paramount, she hurriedly
snapped her handbag closed and went into the other
room.

The bed still seemed to dominate the room and she
was glad to hear the man saying, 'Come and sit down,'
giving her a fair indication that he didn't intend
they should go to bed straight away.

She was glad about that, she thought, as she sat opposite him in one of the chairs. Glad he was more subtle,
glad he wasn't the grabbing type.

'I forgot to ask your name,' he said easily, having no trouble in finding his voice, whereas nerves were
keeping her silent.

'It-it's B-Bunny,' she said, and knew he was aware
she was lying, but suddenly wanting to remain as
anonymous as she had thought he had earlier.

She saw for the first time a small smile of amusement
showing on his face. The smile made her feel calmer,
she felt her nerve ends relax; perhaps it wasn't going
to be so bad after all. He looked different when he
smiled, younger somehow, about thirty-four or five.

'I d-don't know your name either,' she said, and she too smiled when he said:

'Well, Bunny, how about—Wolf?'

'How do you do, Wolf,' she said, feeling astonishingly lighthearted. Her smile disappeared when he stood up and left his chair. Oh no, she thought, he is going to make a grab for me after all. But he didn't, and she breathed in deeply as he passed her chair and she heard the clink of glass.

'I've only whisky here, but I can send down for something else if you prefer . . . ?'

'Whisky will be fine.' She would rather have a lemonade, but didn't want to make a fuss.

He came round to the front of her. 'Here's to you, then, Bunny,' he said, and handed her a glass with a measure of whisky in it.

'Cheers,' she replied with a bravado she wasn't feeling.

He didn't appear to be in any hurry to down his drink, but sat looking at her, his look speculative. 'You looked different downstairs,' he said suddenly.

'Different?' Amber adopted the brittle tone she had heard coming from her lips earlier. She didn't want to go home to sleep alone if he was having second thoughts, to know that the moment she closed her eyes her thoughts and dreams would take on nightmare proportions. 'How different?'

'You're not as hard as I first thought you,' he said slowly, then consideringly, 'Tell me, do you do this sort of thing often?'

'You mean come up to a man's hotel bedroom for a drink?' Her eyes flicked towards the bed, and while covertly watching him she saw his eyes had followed the movement of her to the bed. To hide her nervousness she took another sip of her drink. 'It's not the first time,' she lied, knowing he would know she had lied once they were in that bed together, but desperate that he shouldn't turn her away if the uncanny suspicion that had formed in her mind proved to be correct, that he would find little satisfaction in taking an inexperienced woman to bed.

'Come over here,' he said suddenly.

'I haven't finished my drink yet,' she came back hurriedly, wondering how long she could delay the moment. 'I didn't think you were the grabbing sort.'

'I'm in no hurry,' he told her. 'Take your time with your drink.'

Relief flowed through her for these few minutes' respite, and she turned her head up to smile at him, only to find that his face seemed hazy, and no matter how hard she tried to get him into focus, his outline just wouldn't come clear. She turned her eyes away, looked towards the bed—it swam dizzily in front of her. Was she drunk? She didn't think so. Was this it? she wondered. Was she going to die here in his room? Hadn't she got six months after all? Abruptly she stood up, the room swayed about her.

'What's the matter?'

His voice came to her from quite close by, and she knew he had left his chair and was standing close to her. Needing the comfort of physical contact, she turned, took a step forward and came up against him. Instinctively she laid her head against him, peace washing over her at his solid strength.

'What's the matter?' he repeated, when she didn't want him to say anything.

'Nothing ...' she started to say, then because it must be obvious to him that there was. 'Just hold me,' she pleaded. 'Hold me—love me.'

'The thought had crossed my mind to do something of the sort,' he said, his voice easy. 'But we have all night, and I think I would appreciate you more if you were sober.'

She hadn't meant she wanted him to love her in that way, but how could she expect a perfect stranger, one whom she had been playing up to more or less since she had set eyes on him, to know that the love she wanted was the love she was missing in her orphaned state? She tried to force a laugh that he should think she had had too much to drink, but it died in her throat. 'I'm not drunk,' she denied, and improvised, quickly she thought, for everything was still hazy around her. 'I went to the dentist late this afternoon— the effects of his injection plus whisky made me go dizzy for the moment, but I'm fine now, honestly I am.'

'In that case ...' She felt his head coming down and knew he was going to kiss her.

'D-Do you mind if I go to the bathroom first?' she said quickly on rising panic. 'My mouth feels nasty after the dentist—I'd like to use your toothpaste, if I may.'

Her head felt hot when she made it to the bathroom, and she put a hand up, finding her forehead damp. She was in a blue funk and she knew it. But strangely not at the thought of going to bed with him, but more from knowing he would get scant satisfaction when he found he had an untried girl in bed with him. She knew she wasn't thinking clearly and wished the bathroom would stand still. A sudden feeling of claustrophobia hit her, the small white-tiled room crowding in on her and she knew she had to get into the other room before she fainted.

She was aware of the man she knew as Wolf coming towards her as she came out of the bathroom. The name Wolf made her want to laugh.

'Here I am, Wolfie,' she said in a voice that didn't

sound like her own. 'Your little Bunny is ready and waiting for you.'

The room swayed violently, and she thought she was going to hit the floor with a bump. Then strong arms were around her, and from a long way off she heard him say, 'Here you are indeed, my little Bunny—and I think it's high time that bed was made use of.'

Amber awoke slowly. She didn't know the room she was in, and thought for a moment that she was back in hospital. Then her eyes roved about the room, and she saw a dress she recognised as her own hanging on the outside of the wardrobe. Then she knew exactly where she was—remembered how she had got there, and there her memory faded out. What had happened since was a complete blank. She had no recollection at all of getting into this bed, no recall at all of anything that had taken place. A feeling of alarm gripped her. Had it been such a horrifying experience that hysterical amnesia had set in? She had read of people losing their memory when something very terrible happened and the brain took over and erased it from the mind.

Wide awake now, she turned her head to see that the man who had taken her from girlhood to womanhood was lying with his back to her, and as her eyes widened to see his broad naked shoulders, the thought tumbled in that apart from the bed covers, the rest of him was naked too. A great fear made itself known, and she felt to see if she too was naked. It was small relief to feel she was still wearing her petticoat—had she taken it off and put it on again afterwards?—she couldn't remember. Worse, the thought rushed in, had the man she knew only as Wolf put her into it, or had he made love to her without removing it at all?

The next instant, her face scarlet, Amber slid from beneath the covers. She had to get out of here—get out of here, and now, before he woke up. Suddenly it was imperative that she didn't have to look him in the face again. Shame at what she had done surged through her. She would have a hard time meeting her own eyes in the mirror, let alone see the scorn and contempt that would be in his eyes.

She darted a look across the room. Had she placed her dress so neatly on the hanger—or had he? Again hot colour surged through her cheeks at the thought, and she tiptoed towards the wardrobe praying that the floorboards wouldn't creak and disturb the man whose lust she had satiated.

The coat-hanger made a faint clicking sound as she got it down, and fearfully, holding her breath, Amber looked towards the bed. He stirred in his sleep and she was arrested for a split second that there was none of the harshness in his face she had witnessed last night. In repose that hard look had left him and his mouth was eased out of the controlled lines it had been. Had she put that satisfied curve there? The thought shot through her, and panic-stricken again that her fear of dying had so demoralised her that she had forgotten her upbringing, her parents' gentle teaching that you only gave yourself where love was, she quickly got into her dress, found her shoes and bag and was through the door into the corridor outside, feeling sick that she was so lacking in character she had gone under without putting up a fight.

Amber barely remembered getting home. Automatically she had somehow found a taxi—she had no idea of the time other than that it was still early. But even if there had been a bus that would take her past her door at this early hour, she just couldn't face seeing anyone on that bus who might know her. On reaching her home she went straight to the bathroom, her intention to sit in the bath and try to scrub herself clean, while

knowing that no amount of soap and water would do
that for her. She was horrified when she caught a
glimpse of herself in the mirror. What must the taxi
driver have thought? She looked revolting! She had gone
to bed without removing her make-up and her eyes had
the look of grimed-in mascara on top and bottom
lids—perhaps she had rubbed her eyes at some stage, she
couldn't remember.

Tears mingled with the mascara making her look
more hideous than ever, and angry with herself, Amber
filled the wash basin and scrubbed at her face, removing every trace of the caked-on make-up. How long
she sat in the bath she didn't know. But she came to,
the bath water cold, to hear the phone ringing downstairs. She felt a familiar niggle of pain as she attempted
hurriedly to get out of the bath, but she ignored it
quickly and donned a robe, anxious to answer the
phone, hear another voice who might keep her tortured
thoughts at bay for even a few minutes.

'Amber?' queried the female voice she didn't recognise at the other end. 'Is that Amber Newman?'

'Yes.'

'Sally here. You took your time getting to the phone
—Where were you? In the bath?'

'I was, actually,' Amber answered, not feeling too
pleased with Sally Smith—if she had met her as arranged last night, she wouldn't have . . .

'Sorry I didn't turn up last night—hope you didn't
wait too long.'

'That's all right,' Amber told her coolly. No one was
going to know what Sally Smith's non-arrival had led
to, though she hadn't thought Sally would have the
decency to ring up to apologise. 'Thank you for ringing,' she tacked on politely since Sally had made the
effort to remember her manners.

'Oh, I didn't ring up just for that,' Sally said blithely,

then went on excitedly. 'I've got some good news and when I got down to thinking of whom I could tell, I realised there are very few people I know who would be all that interested.'

Amber wished she could feel she was all agog to hear what Sally was bursting to tell her, but because it wasn't in her to tell her she wasn't interested either, she put a note of friendly enquiry into her voice and asked what her news was.

'I'm getting married,' Sally almost shrieked down the phone. 'Isn't it marvellous! Ray came round while I was getting ready to meet you last night.' Sally went on gibbering on about her 'Ray' while Amber was still trying to sort out how Sally could think of going on a pub crawl while being so madly in love with him, until Sally told her she and Ray had had an enormous row a month back and she hadn't seen him since. And it came to Amber then that Sally, not unlike her, had been attempting to hide her innermost thoughts in any way she could.

'I am pleased for you,' she said sincerely. She didn't know the heartache of being unhappily in love herself, but knew something of heartache, and was truly glad for the girl.

'It is marvellous, isn't it—though,' Sally hesitated, 'I don't know that Ray would have proposed if I hadn't told him that I was pregnant.'

'Pregnant?' Amber wasn't so much shocked that Sally was putting the cart before the horse and getting pregnant first and married second, more shocked because she had thought Sally knew it all, and it was always, she thought, the quiet unassuming types who got themselves pregnant out of wedlock, rather than Sally who she had thought had been born knowing her way around.

'Lovely, isn't it?' Sally trilled. 'Well, I must dash,

Amber. I've got to go and sign on at the unemployment office.'

Amber put down the phone wishing she could treat life in the same uncaring way Sally appeared to—she blocked off her thoughts that she'd left it a little late to adopt some of Sally's carefree attitude, in less than six ... No, she'd never be like Sally anyway, and for all she wished Sally all the luck in the world, she had no desire to be like her. She was more the quiet unassuming type she had thought of when Sally had been speaking to her, the type who got themselves pregnant because they didn't know their way around ... Pregnant! ! !

The word hammered in with such fury, Amber's powers of thinking ceased altogether, before the alarming possibility caused her to all but collapse into the nearest chair. What had she done? Even now she could be pregnant. The thought was so frightening she wanted to be sick. She had no idea if he, Wolf, had taken any precautions, and racked her brains trying to recall something of what had taken place when she had climbed into bed with him. But her amnesia was total. He probably hadn't given the matter any thought. She was certain of that suddenly since if she had been the type of girl he thought she was, he would naturally have assumed she was on the Pill or something. One thing was for sure, she couldn't go along to the hotel and ask for him. She looked at the clock above the fireplace. Half past nine. He would have left the hotel by now anyway, and all she knew about him was that he was unmarried, lived 'not too far away', and the ridiculous name he had dreamed up.

Realising she was shivering, Amber went and got dressed. The pain in her back told her she ought to take a couple of pain-killers, but as she picked up her handbag intending to extract the small bottle, a thought stayed her hand. What if the medication she was on harmed the baby?

Convinced by now she was expecting a child, Amber knew she had to have some help, have some help or end it all now—yet how could she think of ending it, harming something that had already started to grow inside her? Half fainting with panic and fear, she dialled James Cresswell's number, and was answered by his receptionist. The receptionist's cool, impersonal tones helped her to bite down on her panic.

'Is Dr Cresswell free?' asked Amber.

'He's taking surgery.'

'Oh,' she needed to talk to Uncle James, and urgently. 'Amber Newman here,' she identified herself, and then, her control disappearing, 'I need to see him,' she went on, swallowing hard on tears that threatened to choke her, and not waiting for any more she put the phone back on the receiver. Uncle James' receptionist knew her, perhaps she would tell him she had called. Amber didn't think her shaking limbs would get her as far as his surgery if she attempted to go on foot.

When she saw James Cresswell's car pull up outside about an hour later, she raced to the front door and had it standing wide before he had the front gate open.

The smile that had been on his face as he saw her standing there vanished rapidly as he came up to her and saw her ashen, tear-ravaged face. 'My dear!' he exclaimed, his concern showing as he pushed her inside and closed the front door on the outside world. 'Whatever is the matter?'

'Oh, Uncle James,' Amber sobbed, and went into the semi-circle of his arm as he guided her into the sitting room.

'Are you in pain?' he asked, trying to keep his voice impersonal and professional but finding it difficult when observing the state the dear daughter of his two much loved friends was in.

Amber's back was giving her hell, but that was the least of her worries just then. 'It's to be expected, isn't it?' she said, struggling for control.

'Yes,' James Cresswell said slowly. 'But it won't always be as bad as this. In no time you'll find you're as good as ever you were. Just try to ride with it, Amber —your back took a load of punishment, you can't expect it to come right in five minutes.'

'It's not going to come right, though, is it?' she questioned, not waiting for his answer because she knew he wasn't going to tell her the truth. 'I know I'm not going to get better, Uncle James,' she said, and couldn't quite believe that she felt much calmer now it was out in the open. She hoped the calm would stay with her when she told him about her pregnancy.

'Of course you're going to get better.' His eyes moved over her face, his professional glance telling him she was on the verge of nervous collapse.

'Don't lie to me, Uncle James,' she pleaded.

'I'm not lying, Amber,' he said, adopting a stern tone for her benefit. 'By this time next year your back will be as good as new—long before, if you don't do anything silly.' Amber went to interrupt him, but he shushed her to hear him out. 'You've been through a terrible and heartrending experience, my dear. I didn't like the idea of your coming here alone—should have insisted you came and stayed with me for a while.' His voice softened. 'I know you're missing your parents— we all are. They were fine people, Amber, and coping with losing them and the pain that I know pain-killers can't completely deaden has worn you out so that you've let your imagination run riot.' The respect Amber had always had for him had kept her quiet while he finished what he wanted to say to her, but as he concluded, 'Now I'm going to give you an injection

that will ...' she couldn't stay quiet any longer. She
was on her feet before he had finished telling her what
the injection would do for her.

'I know I'm going to die,' she said, cutting across his
words. 'I heard Mr Phillips say at the hospital that he
didn't think I would live longer than six months.'

It was out. Said. Whatever Uncle James had been going to placate her with was unspoken, and Amber
turned away, not wanting to see the shock in his eyes
that she knew what was to be her fate. There was a
moment or two of silence, when neither of them said
anything, then she heard his voice—shocked, certainly,
but not shocked from knowing that she knew, but
shocked at what she had been believing all this time.
He pulled her down into her chair again.

'Listen to me, Amber,' he told her seriously. 'I'm
your G.P. and I would know if anyone would. The injuries you sustained from that rock fall are not terminal. You're going to *live*.' He gave her a gentle shake as
her eyes gazed back in disbelief. 'You have my word
on it. I swear by the love I had for your parents—the
injuries to your back will heal, *you are going to get
well*.'

There was no disbelieving him, yet the idea had become so firmly entrenched in her mind over these last
weeks that she couldn't shake it off, not just like that,
not even with Uncle James swearing on the love he
had for two people she knew he had held so very dear.

'But I heard Mr Phillips say ...'

'I don't care what you heard Mr Phillips say. I have
his note in your file back in my office—I'll show it to
you if you want further proof—it says given care a complete recovery will be made. Now tell me everything
you remember when you heard Mr Phillips make that
remark.'

When James Cresswell had left her, he had gone

without the need to administer his injection after all.
It had been more than a shot in the arm to first
hope, then finally be convinced that she had made a
ghastly and terrible mistake. All the terror that had
beset her on hearing Mr Phillips' words had been for
nothing, for on hearing the whole story from her, James
Cresswell had phoned the hospital straight away, had
spoken with the same ward Sister who had been in
charge when Amber had been there, had listened to
what she had to tell him, put what Amber had told
him to her, and then asked the ward Sister to repeat
everything to Amber. He had handed the phone over
to her and Amber had come away from the phone with
fresh tears streaming down her face—but this time they
had been tears of relief and hope.

'She said that while I was still sedated they'd brought
in an elderly lady who had severe injuries—it must
have been that poor lady Mr Phillips was talking about.
Sister said that when the lady's relatives heard Mr
Phillips' verdict they wanted her to have the best of
everything, and insisted she had private nursing—she
was moved while I was still under the effects of the injection they'd given me. Oh, Uncle James, I feel such
an idiot!' and then, remembering, 'That's why those
screens were there!' It all fitted suddenly. Those screens,
she saw now, had nothing to do with any quirk of
personality Mr Phillips might have. 'They wouldn't
have bothered with those screens had I been the only
patient in that side ward, would they?' She didn't need
to see him shake his head for confirmation.

'So now you're finally convinced, are you?' He was
smiling, and it was all too much for her. She threw
herself into his arms and received his warm, fatherly
hug before he had left her.

One couldn't go through an experience like that and
come out unchanged, Amber thought a week later.

Somehow along the way she had grown up, and it had little to do with the fact that she was now pregnant. She hadn't got round to telling Uncle James about that, though she would soon enough because since she wanted her baby to be perfect, she was going to heed his advice every step of the way. She knew losing her parents had been in part some of the reason for her growing up—she had never had to fend for herself before. But she knew inwardly that should she ever again have the same pronouncement made about her that she had thought Mr Phillips had made, she was now grown up enough to cope with it without panicking and forcing herself to be something she was not. Whatever happened in the future, nothing would induce her to act like the harpy she had that night she had let herself be picked up by Wolf.

Still being unfit to return to work, she had a lot of time to think, and during that week she made up her mind about several things. Since she couldn't hope to hide the fact that she was pregnant, and she didn't think old Mr Turner would take very kindly to having a pending unmarried mother in his office when she was fit to return to her job, she would telephone him and thank him for keeping her job open for her, but say she would not be returning. She had some savings that would see her through for a while, and her parents' estate should be settled by the time the baby arrived, and although her parents had not left her a fortune, there would be enough there if she was careful to enable her to stay at home until her child was perhaps two or three years old.

Mr Turner was very kind when she told him she wouldn't be coming back. 'I don't mind keeping your job open for you until your spine is stronger,' he told her, accepting without question her statement that her doctor felt it unwise for her to sit at her typing desk for any length of time. 'Perhaps you could come in part-time until you're stronger?'

Amber rang off with a feeling of guilt that she had dragged Uncle James' name in as her excuse, for all he had said something along those lines, mixed with a feeling of pleasure that Mr Turner thought well enough of her to suggest the concession of part-time work. Turner, Turner & Scott were old-fashioned enough not to consider taking on part-time employees.

When a week later Amber discovered she was not pregnant after all, she was quite upset. All her plans for having a child on which to shower her love disintegrated, and it was a few days before she came out of her melancholy to realise it was all for the best. And as another couple of weeks went by, each day showing an improvement in her physical condition and with the pain in her back diminishing, for all some of the scars would be with her for ever, so her sleep became less stressful. The nightmares she dreaded became fewer and fewer and at last she believed wholeheartedly that she was going to make a complete and absolute recovery, and she began to realise how much good work everyone had put in to bring that happy state to pass.

She now felt ready to look for some form of employment, but wasn't in any hurry to do anything that would undo the healing processes so far. Only now as she looked back did she realise what a mess she had been. But she wasn't going to look back any more; her sights were set on the future, and although she still missed her parents dreadfully, she knew they would never be at rest if she continually fretted for them.

Accordingly, she scanned through the local paper looking for some form of paid employment, and when she spotted an advert for temporary clerical staff needed by a firm of cardboard box manufacturers who had moved into the area and were wanting staff to help in the transition period, she telephoned for an interview, thinking, a temporary job would suit her down to the ground until she was fully fit to return to the secretarial work she had been trained for.

Mr McGilly, the man who interviewed her for the job, asked about her experience, and didn't seem too keen on taking her when he heard she had been working as a confidential secretary. 'We're not paying that sort of salary,' he underlined.

'I don't expect to receive the salary you would pay a secretary,' Amber replied, having thought Brewsters looked a rather poky outfit, and digging in her heels at the chagrin she felt that they were ready to turn her down. 'I've been ill for a few months and don't want the strain returning to secretarial work would involve for a while,' she told him.

Instantly Mr McGilly's attitude changed and he confided that his wife had recently suffered a nervous breakdown and everyone had been so kind to her that if he could extend that kindness to someone who had suffered the same trauma, he would be pleased to do so.

'You'll soon have your confidence back,' he assured her, making her want to squirm that he was now being so nice to her, his sudden undeserved sympathy making her feel awful, but since he had let his hair down and confided about his wife, she hadn't the heart to tell him he had mistaken the nature of her illness. 'In no time you'll feel able to tackle secretarial work and any stresses that go with it,' he told her, smiling. He then went on to tell her how much the clerical job paid, and when Amber didn't blanch that it was a very poorly paid job, he told her she could start on Monday.

It was a relief to get out of the stuffy office and make her way home. As she sat on the bus and it trundled along, some of the guilt she was feeling fell away. She looked at her reflection in the window as the bus stopped for traffic at a dark hoarding, and wondered if the mark of the mental anxieties she had recently been through was apparent on her face. She owned then that although she hadn't actually suffered a nervous breakdown, thank heaven, it had been a very near thing. She smiled at the long brown-haired reflection that looked back at her, her even white teeth in evidence, then closed her mouth in case anyone was watching her. The only way now was up. She was going to look towards the future—she had already made a start.

CHAPTER THREE

ARRIVING at Brewsters on Monday, Amber was left in charge of a smartly turned out fair-haired girl about her own age. 'Helen will show you the ropes,' said Mr McGilly, giving her an encouraging smile before hurrying away.

'Always up to his eyes in it,' Helen Kempsey remarked, showing Amber to the desk that was to be hers, and instructing her in the use of an antiquated adding machine before giving her a sheaf of papers with columns of figures that had to be added up.

Amber quickly got into the routine of the work, which, busy though they were, was not exacting, there being time for the odd minute or two to get acquainted with the four other girls seated at desks similar to hers, and because every hour or so she had to take her work along to a small pool of typists, it meant her back didn't have chance to set through sitting too long.

By the end of the first week she was on first-name terms with the other girls she worked with, and getting on well with them. But since Helen Kempsey seemed to be more on her own wavelength than any of the others, the two girls gravitated towards friendship. The others were all married and seemed more interested in the price of meat and veg than anything else, and were only there to earn a little extra towards Christmas, which was less than three months away.

Amber wondered about Helen in those first days, because the girl was always expensively turned out and couldn't have afforded to dress the way she did on the money Brewsters paid. She wondered, too, if Helen had

had the sticky time she had in getting Mr McGilly to take her on. Helen had told her one lunch hour that she had only been there a month herself, and at Amber's look of surprise, she had added, 'I'm only in charge of the section by virtue of the fact that I was here a couple of days before any of the others started.'

'Oh,' said Amber, then because it was true, 'Well, you're making a jolly good job of it.'

'Honestly—do you think so?' Helen seemed remarkably pleased at Amber's statement, and confessed, 'Actually, this is the first job I've ever had.' She then seemed to regret having said that. 'You won't tell the others?'

'Of course not,' Amber assured her.

She would have liked to know more about why Helen, who had told her she was the same twenty-two that she was, had not worked before, but she squashed her curiosity. She hadn't told anyone at Brewsters, apart from Mr McGilly, that she had been a secretary. That had been mainly because she had thought that to do so might bring forth questions as to why then was she stuck there doing a humdrum job. She didn't want to tell anyone about the injury to her back in case it got to Mr McGilly's ears and he discovered the real nature of her illness. She felt guilty enough as it was at having got the job because he thought she had suffered a nervous breakdown; she didn't want him to feel put out at having falsely confided in her.

As the weeks slipped by she and Helen became firm friends, though after finding that neither of them had parents, they never spoke about their home backgrounds apart from Helen telling her when she learned that Amber had been an only child:

'I'm luckier than you, Amber—I do have two brothers,' then half to herself, 'though sometimes I could do without them!'

Amber gathered from that remark that occasionally

there were family squabbles, and regretted for the first
time that she had been an only child. It would have
been nice to have a sister or a brother to confide in.
She thrust the thought from her; no one could have had
a happier childhood than she had had.

Often during the following weeks as Christmas drew
near, the two girls would stay in town and have a meal,
and Helen would afterwards drop Amber off at her
home. Amber never questioned how Helen could afford
to keep her car on the road; it was none of her business.

The week before Christmas Helen asked her what she
was doing over the festive season. 'I expect you have one
or two parties to go to?' she questioned.

'Actually, no,' Amber replied, then because that
sounded as though she would be sitting at home twid-
dling her thumbs, 'Uncle James—you remember I
mentioned him a couple of times—he's asked me to go
and stay with him over the holiday . . .'

'He's a doctor, isn't he?' Although she didn't say so,
Helen's tone implied that she didn't think staying with
a fatherly doctor over the festive season was going to be
a barrel-load of laughs.

'Mm, that's right,' Amber confirmed. 'He's a real
love.' He was too. As busy as he was he made a point of
often calling to see her, no longer in the role of her
G.P., although he always asked after her progress, but
as the good family friend he had always been.

They were walking down the High Street, Amber
having thought the subject finished with, then out of
the blue Helen said, 'Why don't you come and stay
with us?'

'Oh, I couldn't!' It came out automatically. Helen's
family wouldn't want her intruding.

'Why not?' Helen's generous mouth firmed in a line
that wasn't to be argued with. 'We'd love to have you.

If you go to your Uncle James, I'll bet you won't see much of him.'

That was true. Being a doctor with a large practice, even if he did have a partner, meant Uncle James could be called out at any time, though she got on well with his housekeeper, Mrs Paget, and she ...

'Look, let's go and have a coffee or something, and discuss it,' said Helen, and Amber found herself seated in a café with her. Helen was determined once she had made up her mind that Amber would be joining her and her brothers at their home at Eldridge Bank, and was ready to knock down any obstacle Amber could put in the way.

'But your brothers won't want me there,' Amber protested. 'They don't know the first thing about me— they might not even like me—what then?'

'Rot,' said Helen. 'Simon will fall for you like a ton of bricks—he's rather partial to good-looking girls, and when he sees the way the light on your hair turns it to amber he'll be sunk without trace.' Amber had to smile at this piece of exaggeration, but sobered when Helen went on, 'It was a brilliant piece of foresight when your parents named you Amber—it fits you exactly with your hair the colour it is when the light shines on it.'

'My mother had the same colour hair,' Amber said quietly. 'I think Mum and Dad were hoping I would inherit it.' Then to get off a subject that was still too new not to be painful, 'What about your other brother?' she asked with forced brightness. 'Will he be sunk without trace too?'

There was a moments pause before Helen answered. 'Er—Dyson's a different kettle of fish,' she said slowly, and sensing she was undoing all the good work she had done so far, 'He's my stepbrother, actually—twelve years older than Simon and me—we're twins, by the

way, but nothing like each other to look at—but I'm
sure he'll like you too.'

Something unsaid in what Helen was saying about
her stepbrother Dyson had Amber sure she wouldn't
like him. 'I think I'd better stick to my original
plan ...' she began.

'Oh, Amber, please,' Helen broke in. 'It's not a spur-
of-the-moment invitation, honestly it isn't. I've been
thinking about it for a week or so now, only to tell you
the truth we won't be doing anything very special and
I thought it might be a little dull for you.'

There was no doubting her sincerity, but Amber
wasn't sure—Uncle James would be the first to tell her
to go and mix with people of her own age group. She
was certain he wouldn't be offended if she didn't stay
with him, but ...

'Please come, Amber,' Helen said again, then after a
moment's hesitation, 'I wasn't going to say anything,
but you'd be doing me a favour if you would come.'

'Favour?' queried Amber.

'Well, yes. I'd better explain a bit about us—I
haven't said much before because—well, family
squabbles are a bit private, aren't they? But the last
time Simon was home from university he and Dyson
had one hell of a row. I thought Dyson was going to
murder him, you could hear the pair of them all over
the house. I went in to try and help and it ended up
with me taking sides with Simon, for all,' she put in,
'I knew he was in the wrong to do what he did, but
he's my twin after all.' She looked at Amber and gave
her a half smile. 'If you're thinking two against one
isn't very fair, don't give it another thought. Dyson
could take half a dozen of us on and still flatten the
lot of us. Anyway, the upshot of the row was that Dyson
laid into me for interfering, saying he would listen to
anything I had to say when I'd deigned to get my

dainty hands dirty and knew something about the word work—he said a lot more besides, but I won't offend your ears by repeating it.'

Amber gathered it must have been one hell of a row. 'So you decided to take a job just to prove ...'

'That's right. I was livid at the time. All stewed up with an "I'll show you" attitude. Though since I wasn't trained to do anything very much other than pour tea into dainty china, I had a devil of a job getting anybody to take me. Had to tell a few fibs to get Mr McGilly to take me,' she confided.

Amber was intrigued by everything Helen was saying. They had never had much more than the occasional grumble in her famly and the few tiffs they'd had were soon made up—the row Helen was talking about sounded like all-out warfare.

'So you showed your brother Dyson that he couldn't talk to you like that and get away with it?' She still had no clear idea what had instigated the row, but couldn't help admiring Helen's spirit.

'Yes,' Helen agreed, then went on, 'Now do you see why you'd be doing me a favour if you came and stayed with us over Christmas?'

Amber wasn't sure that she did. From what Helen had said, she assumed they were a pretty volatile family. She had no idea where Eldridge Bank was; it certainly wasn't around here. If she did take Helen up on her offer, was there anywhere she could run to for cover once the fur began to fly?

Helen saw the doubt in her face. 'Dyson hasn't seen Simon since that row,' she told her. 'After the row Dyson slammed out of the house and when he didn't come home that night, Simon decided to make himself scarce in case whichever girl-friend Dyson had spent the night with hadn't sweetened him up any—not that his temper lasts for very long,' she hastened to assure her,

'but it probably still niggles him at what Simon did—
but he's too self-controlled to let fly at Simon while we
have a guest in the house.'

Helen's simple invitation now seemed much more
complicated than Amber had first thought, and she
didn't quite believe that just the fact of her being there
meant that harmony would reign over the house while
she was there.

'Do come,' Helen urged. 'I promise you Dyson will
be the perfect gentleman while you're around—won't
raise his voice once.'

'How can you be so sure?' Amber wasn't convinced,
and Helen went on to explain:

'My father died a year or so before my mother—I was
fifteen when she died, and went through a bad patch,
latching on to the oddest people as friends. Anyway,
after Dyson had caught me smoking with a group of
them—in a bus shelter of all places!—he insisted I
bring all my friends home to be introduced to him. He
was perfectly charming to everyone of them even
though there were one or two definite thugs among
them, and gradually—I didn't realise it until much
later—he steered me clear of the bad elements until I
was over the bad patch.' Helen laughed reminiscently.
'I shall never know what method he used to get rid of
the baddies, but they dropped out of sight pretty smartish, while the others in the group were always made
welcome. What I'm trying to say, Amber, is that while
Dyson no longer has a need to vet my friends, he'll be
able to tell after one look at you that you're an ideal
friend for me, and I just know he'll do everything in
his power to make your stay with us enjoyable.'

Amber warmed to the sincerity in Helen's tones, and
felt herself being won over. Dyson didn't sound so very
terrible after all. She knew she wasn't a 'thug' or a
'bad element'. A picture of the man Wolf flashed

through her mind, as it often did, to be quickly rejected. Surely everyone was allowed one lapse?

'I'll come,' she said quickly before the picture of that dark, morose man could come back again.

'Oh, good.' There was no doubting Helen's pleasure as she got down to organising the details.

Eldridge Bank, Helen explained, was a small village about thirty miles away on the edge of Exmoor. It seemed a long way for Helen to travel to come to work at Brewsters, but she explained that she didn't want anyone locally to know she had a job, the same pride showing that had made her get a job in the first place.

Brewsters were closing down on Tuesday until the following Monday, so it was arranged that Helen would drive Amber to her home on Tuesday to pick up her case after work and drive her to Eldridge Bank.

Amber was in a dilemma as to whether or not to buy presents for Simon and Dyson. She had never met them and didn't expect them to buy her anything, but knew she would die of embarrassment if they had and she had nothing to give in return. She pondered the matter for some time, then decided she *would* get them something. It would act as a thank-you present for having her to stay as well. Having purchased two very nice ties, a discreet blue one for Dyson who Helen had said had dark hair, and a green one for Simon, whose hair according to Helen was a 'mucky red colour', Amber parcelled them up and stuck the 'Best Wishes' labels on. A present for Helen had been no problem because she already knew the name of Helen's favourite perfume, and expensive though it was, she thought nothing was too good for Helen allowing her into the circle of her family.

She had presents for Uncle James and Mrs Paget too, and after ringing Mrs Paget first and finding that Uncle James was not on call that night, the Thursday before

Christmas she took her presents to his house. Mrs Paget let her in, telling her the doctor was in the sitting room, and Amber handed Mrs Paget the present she had for her, neatly wrapped in its Christmas wrapping. She knew Mrs Paget had a weakness for anything glass and hoped she would be pleased with the unusually shaped glass candle-holder complete with its matching candle.

'Let me have your coat,' said Mrs Paget. 'I've a present for you too, Amber,' and they both laughed as they said together, 'Not to be opened until Christmas.'

Amber found James Cresswell listening to some of his favourite records. She went quietly into the sitting room and one glance at the well worn battered slippers on his feet was sufficient for her to be pleased she had selected a pair of sheepskin-lined slippers for his present.

'I wasn't expecting company,' he said, opening his eyes and becoming aware that he wasn't alone. 'Always a pleasure to see you, Amber—come and sit down.' She saw his glance go to the gaily wrapped parcel she was carrying.

'I—er—I've brought your present round tonight,' she said, placing it down on a low table before seating herself. 'Uncle James, would you mind very much if I didn't spend Christmas with you?' she went on.

'You're not thinking of staying at home by yourself, are you?' he asked, frowning. 'I don't think that's a very good idea, my dear.'

When Amber told him about Helen's invitation to stay with her in Eldridge Bank, his frown disappeared and the sunshine of his smile came through. 'An excellent idea,' he proclaimed. 'I must admit I was looking forward to pulling a cracker with you,' he teased, 'but it will do you far more good to be with someone your own age. What are this Helen and her family like?' he asked, not from any sense of making sure they were respectable folk, but showing a natural interest in her friends.

'I haven't met Helen's brothers—she has two, Simon and Dyson, but she says . . .'

'Dyson? Eldridge Bank?' said James Cresswell, as if trying to make a connection. 'That wouldn't be Dyson Silver, would it?'

Uncle James got around far more than she did, he seemed to know Eldridge Bank at any rate, and Helen's brother too, from what he was saying.

'I don't know, Uncle James. Helen's name is Kempsey, but Dyson is her stepbrother, so his name could be Silver—I never thought to ask. Why, do you know him?'

'I'll bet it's the same chap,' James Cresswell said pensively. 'From all accounts he's quite well-to-do— quite a tycoon around Exmoor way— has his finger in one or two pies round here too, so I've heard.'

Amber remembered that there was no real need for Helen to work for her living, and felt a little apprehensive, half wishing she hadn't accepted the invitation now. It hadn't bothered her before that Helen's clothes had an expensive look to them, and although her own wardrobe was fairly plentiful, very little in it, apart from her sheepskin jacket, had cost a quarter of what Helen must pay for her clothes—how would she fit in to such a well-to-do environment?

'Do you think I shouldn't go after all?' she questioned doubtfully. 'I didn't know Helen's people were that well off.'

'Nonsense,' James Cresswell scoffed. 'You're every bit as good as they are.'

Amber packed the things she would be taking with her on the Monday night, unsure which of her two favourite long dresses to take, so she packed them both. Her best suit she would be wearing to the office tomorrow; there would be no time to change when Helen brought her back to collect her suitcase. She was glad Helen had suggested coming back to pick up her case, for as she added a trouser suit, two calf-length dresses, underwear, jeans and toiletries, not to mention shoes and various other odds and ends, her suitcase was becoming quite heavy, and though lugging it with her on the bus would normally not have bothered her, she had been without pain for a week or two now, and was anxious not to do anything to cause her any discomfort over the holiday.

'I can't say I'm not looking forward to not having to come back here until next Monday,' said Helen, as she steered her car out of the small side street near to Brewsters on Christmas Eve. 'You'd think they were giving us an extra week's pay, the magnanimous way they said we could get off an hour early.'

Amber laughed, mentally agreeing. Other small factories and offices nearby had packed up at lunch time as a concession to the festive season. It didn't take more than ten minutes to reach her home and pick up her suitcase. She invited Helen in, but they didn't stop very long as Helen said it looked like snow, and it would be better to take advantage of their extra hour of freedom.

Helen was obviously looking forward to Christmas, and some of her enthusiasm brushed on to Amber as the car sped along, though she couldn't help wondering if Helen's two brothers had patched up their quarrel.

'Is your brother home from university?' she asked, thinking he must be, but not liking to ask outright the question that had given her a few anxious moments —she was a stranger to a strained atmosphere and didn't know if she was equipped to deal with it.

'Oh yes,' Helen said breezily, and in answer to Amber's unasked question 'All's quiet on the Western Front!'

The house, which went by the simple name of Moor View, was larger than Amber had been prepared for. Dusk had already fallen, but the house still loomed large and imposing. But she had no time to question the disquiet of, would she fit in? for Helen was out of the car saying, 'Come on, Amber—I can't wait for my brothers to get a sight of you—you'll knock 'em for six!'

Heartened by this piece of banter she didn't believe in, Amber followed Helen up the stone steps, glad she hadn't got very far to walk with her case. The hall was already illuminated as they went through the massive front door, and as no one was about, Helen told her to hang on at the bottom of the stairs with her case while she went to see where everyone was. The hall seemed to be quite long with doors going to the right and the left of it, and Amber watched as Helen disappeared through one of the doors to the left. Then before she could do more than glance about her, a door to the right opened and a tall, dark-haired man came out.

He saw her straight away, but even before he started to come towards her, the shock of recognition had Amber feeling she was going to faint. She had already placed her case down by her feet, and she clutched at the newel post of the stairs while praying with all her heart that the hard-looking man approaching her had not in turn recognised her. For the last time she had seen him, her face had been plastered with make-up, and it had been in his hotel bedroom in Exeter.

He came and stood in front of her, his hard eyes looking down into her ashen face—Helen's stepbrother, for he could be no one else, was none other than the man she knew only as Wolf!

He looked at her unsmiling, unspeaking, and while she was still searching for something to say, still hoping he had not recognised her, but doubting it very much, she heard Helen coming back along the hall.

'Oh, there you are, Dyson—I've been looking in the drawing room for you and Simon.'

'Simon's out,' Dyson said smoothly, turning to glance at his stepsister.

Helen came up to them, noticing at once the whiteness of Amber's face. 'Are you all right, Amber—you look ghastly?'

'I'm fine,' Amber replied quickly, not wanting Helen to draw Dyson's attention to her.

'It's the change in the temperatures, I expect,' Dyson was saying urbanely. 'It's bitter cold out and since one always feels cold in another person's house, I've had the heating turned up a degree or two to welcome your friend—I'll have it turned down later.'

There was nothing in his tone to suggest that he had recognised her, and though she was able to relax slightly as the thought penetrated that it was nearly four months since that night and that there must have been quite a few women for this virile-looking man since he had taken her to bed, the nausea remained that she was expected to stay here in the same house with him for almost a whole week.

'That's probably it,' Helen agreed with her step-brother's verdict that the abrupt change in temperatures had been the reason for Amber's wilting appearance. 'I thought it was because you were scared of meeting my family,' she said lightly, 'but . . .'

'I'm sure Amber isn't such a frightened rabbit as all that,' Dyson said smoothly, and fresh shock hit Amber. For at his words, his reference to a rabbit when she had told him her name was Bunny, she knew without a shadow of a doubt that as she had recognised him straight away, he had recognised her.

'Would you like a drink of something first, or would you like to see your room?'

Amber latched on to what Helen was saying. She knew she wouldn't be staying, but for the moment she had to get away from the enigmatic glare of Dyson's eyes.

'My room, I think,' she said, her voice suddenly husky.

'Come on, then.' Helen picked up her case and started up the stairs. 'I'll give you a chance to unpack, and by then Simon should be home and we can all have a go at decorating the Christmas tree.'

Amber went to follow her up the stairs, but found her way blocked by Dyson. Was he going to say here and now, with Helen in earshot, that he didn't consider her a suitable friend for his sister? She recalled Helen saying he no longer vetted her friends, but she didn't lay any credence in that any more. Then he was stepping to one side, giving her an almost imperceptible sardonic bow, but she saw it and colour flared in her face as she followed Helen up the stairs. She would have to tell Helen something as soon as they were alone together—she didn't want to tell her the truth, but somehow she would have to invent a plausible story that would get her back to Exeter tonight.

'Here we are,' said Helen, waiting for her to catch her up and opening one of the many doors along the wide landing. 'Because you're lovely and feminine, I thought you would like a room that's pretty and feminine,' and Amber followed her into a room that was a fairytale delight of femininity. The first thing that caught her eye was the bed, a gorgeous lace and net-draped fourposter.

'Why, it's exquisite!' she breathed, her bewildered

thoughts ousted for a brief while at her friend's
thoughtfulness in thinking she would like this room
with its walls papered in the palest of pinks with a faint
silver stripe going down, the frilled dressing table complete with an arrangement of delicate flowers. 'Oh,
Helen,' she exclaimed, and felt completely overcome
on seeing the flowers, knowing that this was Helen's
way of saying, 'Welcome—we want you to be happy
with us.'

Sensing that Amber was feeling rather emotional,
Helen adopted a think-nothing-of-it manner, though
Amber could see she knew how she felt. 'I'll leave you
to it,' she said. 'Simon would have been here to greet
you—he said so this morning—only none of us knew
Brewsters were going to let us off an hour early.'

After Helen had gone, Amber tore her eyes away from
her beautiful surroundings, a sudden feeling of dull-
ness swamping her. Helen had gone out of her way to
make her welcome, and all she could do to repay her
was to tell her she couldn't stay. She knew it would
sound ungrateful, but there was no way she could con-
template staying in the same house as the stepbrother
Dyson—even supposing he was prepared to let her, and
she had her doubts about that. What had Helen said
that time when she had told her about the friends she
had picked up with after her mother's death? 'I shall
never know what method he used to get rid of the
baddies, but they dropped out of sight pretty smartish.'
She would have to explain something to Helen, Amber realised, but she wasn't waiting around for Dyson
to give her her marching orders.

She left the small bedroom chair she had collapsed
into as soon as Helen had gone, and was on her feet
knowing she would have to seek the other girl out and
tell her she wouldn't be staying after all, but before she
could get to the door she saw the handle turn, and

stood rooted as it opened.

Amber wasn't surprised to see Dyson standing there; she had known deep down that it wouldn't be very long before he chose some moment to have a 'private word' with her, though she would have preferred to have left without having to see him again.

'Thank you for knocking,' she offered, arming herself with sarcasm to get herself over this interview.

'Please forgive my lack of manners,' his tone was mockingly insincere. 'I quite forgot men always knock before they enter your room.'

The barely veiled suggestion that men were no strangers to her bedroom had to be ignored, Amber saw. She had no defence against it, and could see little point in telling him he was the only man who had been allowed that privilege apart from her father and her doctor—he wouldn't believe her anyway.

Dyson Silver closed the door behind him and came further into the room. Then all mockery left him. 'Not unpacked yet, I see.' Her suitcase was still where Helen had left it, no evidence of Amber's possessions on the dressing table or anywhere else.

'A pretty pointless occupation, wouldn't you say, since I'm not likely to be staying.' She saw his eyes narrow at that, and realised with a small spark of pleasure that she had stolen his thunder if he had been ready, as she was sure he was, to tell her to get out.

'You catch on very quickly,' he said, agreeing she wasn't staying.

'Oh, don't worry,' she shrugged airily. 'Though I know little about your family, I know enough to be aware that you think I'm not good enough to associate with Helen.'

'You've been reading my script,' he said insolently. 'There doesn't seem to be a thing I can tell you that you haven't figured out for yourself.'

Amber felt sick at his cool insolence. She had never come across anybody like him before—but suddenly all the blame being placed squarely at her door made her mad. He had been a party to it too, and it just didn't seem fair that she should be the one to be made to squirm when he was as responsible as she was for what had happened.

'Men!' she exclaimed in angry disgust. 'It's all right for you, isn't it? You can have your—fun and think nothing of the consequences, but women ...'

'But there weren't any consequences, were there,' he stated smoothly.

She wished he hadn't interrupted her, she had been getting quite into her stride. But as what he said hit her, and he could only be referring to the fact that she was not pregnant—the evidence of that was before him. Amber bit her lip; she would be nearly four months pregnant by now if there had been any consequences, and she stood before him as slim as a reed.

'No ... no,' she faltered, 'there weren't—but no thanks to you.' She thought he looked a little surprised at that and wondered if he had taken precautions after all, and her face flamed at the thought, so that she turned her head away from him. It was all right for him, he could remember everything that had happened that night, while her memory, mercifully, was still blank. She felt insulted and degraded, and though it was partly her own fault since she had invited his advances that night, she wanted to hit out at him in any way she could. 'Anyway,' she went on, injecting every ounce of scorn of which she was capable into her voice, 'I've had much better lovers than you since that night.'

'I don't doubt it,' he came back, and she could hear the disgust in his voice at the tramp he thought she was. 'But we were hardly lovers, were we?'

'No,' she had to concede, still not looking at him,

'love played no part in it, did it?' Then feeling too nauseated by the whole conversation and thinking she would be sick if the conversation wasn't soon ended, 'There was no need for you to come and throw me out —I'm going.' She turned to face him. His face was impassive, telling her nothing of his thoughts. 'I'll have to see Helen first—but I would rather, if you wouldn't mind, that she doesn't know anything about—about us.'

He studied her for some moments, his eyes passing over her pale face, the halo of amber around her from the electric light above her head, then he turned abruptly without saying a word until he had the door open.

'I'll send Helen up to you—you would much prefer to tell your lies without anyone else being present, I feel sure.'

Amber didn't have to wait very long for Helen to appear. Helen had changed into a shirt and jeans. All ready to decorate the Christmas tree, Amber thought, and felt tears sting the back of her eyes that she would be no part of this family occasion.

'What's up?' Helen asked straight away as she came into the room. 'Dyson tells me you've decided not to stay.'

'I ... Oh ...' She hadn't really thought whether she went or stayed would matter very much to anyone, but the hurt look in Helen's eyes made her feel two feet tall. 'Oh, Helen, I'm sorry. You've been more than kind— given me this lovely room—but I can't stay.'

'Why ever not?' Helen looked ready to be difficult. 'I want you to stay, Amber. You agreed to come as a favour to me—you can't back out now.' And she perched herself on the dressing table stool, and looked ready to sit there for ever unless Amber could give her good reason for not staying.

'I don't think your brother likes me,' Amber blurted out, feeling herself cornered and coming out with the first thing that was the nearest to the truth.

'Dyson?' Helen queried, while knowing Amber hadn't yet met Simon. 'Oh, Amber, if Dyson's attitude has put you off, forget it.' Though Helen looked as though she couldn't remember anything in Dyson's attitude to be very off-putting when the three of them had been down in the hall. 'A lot of people don't take to him straight away, but he's a really warm person when you get to know him. Look,' she went on, before Amber could insert anything, 'I'll get him to come up and have a chat with you—he'll make you see how welcome you are, you see if he doesn't.'

'No, Helen,' said Amber, but she was talking to an open doorway as Helen sped off.

CHAPTER FOUR

AMBER closed the door after Helen had gone, knowing she hadn't managed that very well. She sighed, and took the seat Helen had leapt up from only minutes previously. She had no idea what Helen was saying to her stepbrother, but only hoped Dyson wasn't telling her how she had allowed herself to be picked up by him that night. She thought he would draw a veil over what had followed, but Helen wasn't so dumb that she couldn't fill in the blanks.

It hurt her that by now she would have lost all the respect Helen had for her. The other four girls in the clerical section at Brewsters had left today, and only she and Helen had been kept on. It would be impossible for the two of them to work together with the constraint of knowing she had been easy game for Dyson between them.

She heard a sound of footsteps in the corridor and stood up, placing her handbag over her arm. Any second now that door would open—she only hoped Helen would be civil to her when she asked if she was ready to go. But when the door opened, it wasn't Helen who came through it, but Dyson.

'Well,' he said, closing the door, and leaning against it, 'aren't you the clever one!' Amber looked at him, her face puzzled. 'Come on, Bunny—not stuck for words, surely? Don't you know you're supposed to trot out "I don't know what you're talking about"?'

'I really don't know what you're talking about,' Amber obliged. 'And don't call me Bunny!'

'But my dear,' Dyson said mockingly, 'you told me

yourself your name was Bunny.'

She could do without being reminded of that. 'Well, now you know it isn't,' she snapped. Then as a sinking thought struck her, 'It's not you who's going to drive me home, is it?' She would walk sooner.

'Oh, you're not going home, Miss Newman, believe me—at least not until this jolly festive season is over.'

'I am,' Amber argued. 'I wouldn't dream of spending one night under your roof.'

'Yet you had no objection to spending one night in my bed.'

'That was different.'

'I'll say it was different,' he said, with an emphasis that was lost to her. 'But just to put you in the picture, I've just left a sister downstairs who's very near to tears at the thought that I, the villain of the piece apparently, am acting a little coldly to her waif and stray.'

'I'm not a waif and stray!' Amber burst in angrily, and saw him raise an unconcerned eyebrow as the sparks flew from her eyes. 'And I'm not staying here.'

'Oh, but you are—— You see, Miss Newman, Helen has got it into her head that far from being the cheap little floosie I know you to be, you're a pure and sensitive shrinking violet, a little orphan Annie who needs to be part of our family this Christmastide otherwise you'll have nowhere to go other than stay with some obscure old gentleman she refers to as your "Uncle James" but who I'm sure is more of a sugar-daddy to you . . .'

'Uncle James isn't . . .' Amber started to defend, then closed her mouth as Dyson suddenly tired of baiting her and advanced further into the room to take a firm grip on her shoulders.

'Make up your mind to it, Amber Newman—you're staying. I'm not having Helen sending me sulky glances the whole of the Christmas period because she thinks my attitude to you had driven you away.'

'You haven't told her about . . .'

'About your haste to get into bed with me?' he finished for her, his eyes taking on a thoughtful look that it should worry her. 'Make no mistake, I shan't have the slightest compunction in doing so if you don't play ball.'

'You'll only be blackening yourself.' Amber tried desperately to get through to him the impossibility of her staying.

'Helen knows I'm no saint where the ladies are concerned—though I've never brought one of them under my roof before.'

'There you are, then,' Amber came back, her colour high.

'What do you mean "There you are, then"? You aren't supposing I shall want to repeat that experience back in Exeter, are you?'

Amber broke away from his grip, her face furious. 'How dare you—as if I'd give you the chance!'

'Oh, you'd give _me_ the chance all right. I know your sort—mad for anything in trousers. Just don't play your little games with Simon—keep out of his bedroom while you're here, he's young and impressionable, and I'd hate him to imagine he'd fallen in love with you.'

'You don't fancy me as a sister-in-law?' Amber couldn't stop herself from flinging back, furious that anyone could think she was only one step from the gutter.

'Heaven forbid,' he snapped explosively. 'You keep your wiles for men of your own kind.'

Suddenly Amber had had enough. 'It's impossible for me to stay—don't you see that?' she asked quietly. 'Let me go, Mr Silver . . .'

'Did Helen tell you my name is Silver?'

Amber was put out for a minute, until she realised

they had never been introduced. 'No—Helen seldom talks about her family,' she said, and saw him nod as though thinking that was more in keeping with the Helen he knew. 'That is your name, though, isn't it?'

'Yes,' he confirmed, 'and since Helen didn't tell you, and knowing Helen she's kept quiet about a lot of things—what else have you been able to find out about us?'

She had no idea what he was getting at, but since he had dropped the cynical, mocking tone, she thought there might still be a chance he would agree to her returning to Exeter, she saw no reason not to tell him what Uncle James had told her.

'Uncle James,' she began, and saw his eyes narrow, but thought nothing of it and continued, 'Uncle James said he thought your name must be Silver when I mentioned that I was coming to Helen's home at Eldridge Bank. He said you were well-to-do, and . . .'

'Well-to-do? What do you think *Uncle James* meant by that?'

The way he said *Uncle James* wasn't lost on her, but she couldn't see any reason why he should put emphasis on those two words. 'Well, wealthy I suppose—rich, I imagine.'

'Rich, you imagine,' Dyson Silver repeated. 'And what did your uncle think when you told him you were coming to Moor View to stay?'

'He thought it a good idea,' Amber replied innocently, having lost her interrogator some moments ago. She was completely unprepared when his hands came out again and he took her shoulders in a bruising hold.

'I'll *bet* he thought it a good idea!' he almost spat at her. And as Amber could do nothing but stare at him as if he had suddenly gone mad, her brown eyes grew wide in sudden fear.

'I don't . . .' she began.

'I'm sure you don't,' he interrupted her. 'Why do you think Helen never mentions her family? Why? Because she knews that the three of us—myself, and Helen and Simon when they reach the age of twenty-five—are wide open to fortune-hunters, gold-diggers and the like.'

'And you think I'm a gold-digger?' Amber breathed hoarsely, before rage so blinding, a rage she had never before experienced, was flooding through her, and because his hands were still on her shoulders anchoring her upper limbs, she brought her foot back and kicked him so mightily on the shin, it should have broken in half. She heard his grunt of pain, but was careless of it as he let go his hold on her, leaving her free to yank up her suitcase and tear from the room. One night spent with that pig of a man and he thought he could say what he liked to her—she'd see him in hell before she spent one night in his house!

She had just made it to the top of the staircase when strong arms gripped her and she found her feet were treading the air. She was picked up bodily from behind and carried kicking and struggling with her suitcase back into the room she had just marched from in high dudgeon.

She hit the bed with a bump as a furious-looking Dyson threw her on to it, her case thudding to the floor. A shooting pain in her back robbed her of the words that came hurtling to her lips, but if Dyson was still in pain from that vicious kick she had dealt him, it didn't stop him from voicing his opinion of her and calling her all the names he could lay his tongue to. Amber learned that she was a damned fallacious hell-cat, an irritating shrew, a wild termagant, and he ended with, '... you testy little virago! If it wasn't for the peace and goodwill of the season, I'd take my belt off to you for that!'

'It's a pity I didn't break your leg,' Amber breathed, refusing to be daunted that he looked ready to use his belt, peace and goodwill or not.

They glared at each other, drawing hostility with every breath. Then suddenly Dyson laughed. It was a pleasant sound; even though she thought she hated him, Amber couldn't deny that.

'I think,' he said, his laughter gone from him, but a trace of amusement still playing round the corners of his mouth, 'this should prove one of the most interesting Christmases I've spent in a long time.'

'You surely don't mean you *still* want me to stay?' Amber managed to inject sarcasm into her voice; her anger had faded with his laughter.

'You intrigue me, Amber Newman, looking as if butter wouldn't melt and cheese wouldn't choke,' he said, looking down at her from his lofty height. Then, all amusement disappearing, 'Tramp you certainly are. Gold-digger? Maybe. But I'm sure about one thing: you're certainly going to liven things up around here.'

Me! Amber thought. I'm the quiet, unassuming sort. Well, she qualified; she always had been until she had come into contact with Dyson Silver. She realised, then, that she was beaten. Intrigue him she might, but if she stayed—and it didn't look as if she was going to get away; for the last ten miles of the journey here she had seen barely a soul, so she could be fairly sure they were way off a bus route, and since Dyson had decreed she was staying she wouldn't put it past him to put all the cars at Moor View out of action—but if she stayed, she was sure of one thing; he was going to watch her very closely to see she didn't get her hooks into his brother Simon or run off with the family heirlooms.

She got up from the bed when Dyson Silver left the room. Oh, how she hated him! Her lips firmed together. She wasn't going to cry—he'd love that, wouldn't he, the brute, the bully! She had so looked forward to being part of Helen's family this Christmas too, she reflected, looking moodily at her suitcase, not wanting to unpack but knowing she was going to have to. A quiet time spent at Uncle James' house seemed infinitely preferable now. A tap on her door brought her out of her reverie. She knew it wouldn't be Dyson Siver—he wouldn't knock.

'Come in,' she called.

A young woman entered bearing a tray of tea which she placed down on the bedside table. 'Miss Kempsey said you might be feeling a little thirsty,' the maid told her, adding that her name was Maureen. 'Miss Kempsey thought you might like a hand with your unpacking,' she added, her eyes going to Amber's unopened case.

Amber forced a smile to her lips. Maureen had no part in the gall that welled up in her that Dyson had lost no time in informing his sister that she was staying.

'That's kind of you, Maureen, but I can manage—thank you very much for the tea, though, I could do with a cup.'

Her unpacking didn't take very long, and although it had seemed to her she was bringing half of what she owned, wanting to have something suitable for any occasion that might arise, the things she had brought with her looked lost in the spacious built-in wardrobes that seemed to go on for miles. Since Helen had been wearing jeans, Amber opted to do the same. She would like to help decorate the tree, and since she suspected the room Dyson had come from when she had waited in the hall downstairs must be his study, perhaps if the gods were kind to her, he would spend the evening in there.

Dressed in her newest jeans and snugly fitting white

sweater, Amber picked up the tray Maureen had brought in and made her way downstairs. She could hear laughter coming from the room she now knew to be the drawing room, and hesitated wondering what to do—ought she to try and find the kitchen and deposit the tray first?

The decision was taken from her as the drawing-room door opened and she saw Helen backing out of the room, heard her say, 'You are a clown, Simon,' which told her Simon was home. Then Helen had closed the door and was turning to see her there.

'Ah, Amber, I was just coming to look for you.' She took the tray from her. 'You needn't have brought that down, Maureen would have done it—but come into the kitchen and I'll introduce you to Mrs Randle, our housekeeper.'

Amber followed Helen down the hall, turning to the right at the end to go down a few steps and into a large airy kitchen. Maureen was there along with a couple of other women. Amber thought she had guessed which was the housekeeper, and her guess turned out to be right when Helen introduced her to the small, neat-looking woman who looked to be in her fifties. Amber took to her ready smile.

'And this is Jean,' Helen introduced the other woman, who was the plumpish lady dressed in a green overall.

Helen explained on the way back from the kitchen that they wouldn't be dressing for dinner that night. 'We usually have a makeshift meal on Christmas Eve,' she said. 'Dyson likes to let the staff have as much time off as he can at Christmas, and with a special effort being made for our meals tomorrow he thinks the kitchen staff have got their hands full—besides which,' she confided, 'we're usually too keen to get on with the decorating to want to linger over a meal that will make us feel sluggish afterwards.'

They were outside the drawing-room door when Helen stopped and gave Amber's arm a gentle squeeze. 'I'm so glad you decided to stay,' she said, and there was so much sincerity in her voice, Amber felt mean that she had ever thought of leaving. That was until Helen added, 'Dyson will prove to you over your stay how much he wants you with us.'

Her heart quailed momentarily. Not if he acted the way he had up in her room he wouldn't, she thought, then decided he wasn't likely to let his opinion of her show while she was in company with Helen. And since she risked spoiling Helen's Christmas if she let her see how she felt about him, then she would do everything in her power to hide her feelings, and she would take good care never to be alone with him again.

The drawing room was a delight. Already the walls and picture frames had been decorated with holly. It was a huge room, thickly carpeted, with an assortment of easy chairs, settees and occasional tables, and over by the window, knee-deep in tinsel and fairy lights, stood a young man who Amber knew from Helen's description of his 'mucky' red-coloured hair must be Simon. Dyson was there too, but Amber's glance only flicked in his direction, and he was too far away for her to read the expression in his eyes, though she knew he was taking his fill of her in her jeans and sweater.

'Damn!' said Simon, extricating himself from the tinsel and coming up to them. 'We've already got a fairy for the top—but as I live and breathe you're truly something straight out of my dreams!'

Amber's smile was natural, she wanted to laugh at Simon's statement, but because Dyson was in the room held it back. In direct opposition to his stepbrother, Simon was the most uncomplicated man she had met in a long while.

'This is Simon,' Helen introduced him. 'I should warn you,' she added dryly, 'his shyness gets worse.'

Amber extended her hand to him, and Simon took her hand in his to give her a warm handshake. 'Amber,' he said, keeping hold of her hand and pulling her under the light. 'It suits you. Your hair is like . . .'

'Amber also means "take care".' Dyson's voice broke the moment, and Amber was the only one, she thought, who noticed the sting in Dyson's words, for both Helen and Simon were smiling.

Simon let go her hand. 'I guess you're right, Dyson— as ever,' he tacked on the end. 'A man could lose his heart to such a maiden if he didn't exercise a little caution.'

Amber saw, where the other two did not, the way Dyson's left eyebrow went up a notch at the word 'maiden', and wanted to hit him, feeling herself going crimson at the same time.

'Pack it in, Simon,' Helen put in. 'You're making Amber blush!'

'Sorry.' Instantly Simon was apologetic. 'I didn't know girls blushed any more. Come and see what I'm doing with the tree, Amber.'

By the time dinner was served the tree was more than half finished. It was a massive tree, a smaller one would have been lost in the huge room, and after their meal of soup, cold meat and salad, followed by a fresh fruit salad, they all returned to the drawing room, with Simon declaring they would have a half hour's rest and then tackle the tree again.

Dyson had had very little to say to her, but the remarks he had made had been courteous, and if Amber was looking for a sting in the tail of the few comments that came her way from him, she was having difficulty in finding any. It would appear, she thought, that he was trying to show to them all she was a much welcomed guest in his house, only she wasn't fooled. Still, she reminded herself, if she was able to keep out of his way, the rest of her visit should be able to pass without her attempting to break his leg again. Having a sympathetic nature, she was shaken to think she didn't feel one bit appalled at the heartfelt wish that he had a lump the size of a duck's egg on his shin, and the hope that it was throbbing like the on-off lights of a pedestrian crossing.

'There,' said Simon, when at ten o'clock he sat perched on the top of the ladder steps and placed the fairy on the top of the tree. 'What does it look like from down there?' He was addressing no one in particular, but was looking at Amber.

'It looks beautiful,' Amber said huskily, a feeling of tightness in her throat. Her father had always placed the fairy on the tree last, it was a sort of family ritual. She forced a smile to her lips. 'I'll hold the steps for you if you're ready to come down,' she said brightly.

'I could fall down and neither Helen nor Dyson would bother,' he said with an injured air.

'Well, so long as you fell on your head we'd have nothing to worry about—apart from the hollow echo,' Helen chipped in, and they all laughed, Simon included.

'For that remark, you can go to church tomorrow and beg forgiveness,' said Simon, coming down the steps.

Amber moved away as Simon safely reached the floor. 'Is there a church near here?' she asked.

'There's one in the village—about half a mile away,' Helen told her. 'Just off the main road. Arthur, Mrs Randle's husband, sings in the choir there—he has a beautiful bass voice,' she added.

Amber hadn't seen a village within half a mile of Moor View, so the village must lie in the opposite direction from the way they had come. It was a long-standing tradition in her family that they always went to church on Christmas Eve, and now she knew there was a church nearby, it seemed important to her that she kept faith with her parents, kept the tradition going. But she knew she could not mention it, not while Dyson was in the room. She just couldn't bear to have him mocking her wish to go to church.

At half past ten Helen yawned delicately and said if nobody would mind she was going to bed. Amber was on her feet, saying she thought she would do the same.

'There doesn't seem much for me to stay down for if you're disappearing,' Simon said to Amber, and received a quelling look from his brother for making it so obvious that he had taken to her. 'I know I'm not as subtle as you, brother dear,' said Simon, striking the only sour note of the evening, 'but then I've a long way to go before I can match your experience.'

What Dyson said in answer to that Amber had no idea, for with a brief goodnight to them both, she and Helen left the room.

'I do wish Simon would watch what he says to Dyson,' Helen confided as they went up the stairs. 'He's no match for him when it comes to a battle of words—I expect Dyson will flatten him with a few well-chosen sentences now that we've left them. Thank goodness you're here—they'd be at each other's throats tomorrow if you weren't.'

Amber looked at her and Helen seemed to read the expression on Amber's face that said if she wasn't here, Simon wouldn't have made that remark, and the need for Dyson to 'flatten him' wouldn't have arisen.

'If it hadn't been what Simon said to you, then it would have been something else,' she sighed. 'I thought what happened between the two of them the last time

Simon was home would have blown over by now, but it's only just buried beneath the surface by the look of it—still,' she brightened up, 'with you here they'll remember their manners, and there won't be an explosion until after the holiday is over.'

Amber went to her room feeling glad that she might in some small way have something to contribute, if only by being there, to the peace and goodwill Dyson had spoken of earlier, but her thoughts again returned to James Cresswell and his uncomplicated household.

Ten minutes later she heard footsteps pass her room. That would be Simon, she thought. Then after another few minutes or so she heard the sound of someone else coming to bed. Dyson, she thought, and glanced at her watch. If the service in the church started at half past eleven as she thought it would, she had plenty of time to get there if she started now. Just off the main road, Helen had said, and if Mrs Randle's husband Arthur was singing in the choir, since Helen had told her over dinner that Mrs Randle had a flat in the house, then the doors wouldn't be locked until Arthur was in, would they? At least, she could always come in through the kitchen if the front door was locked.

Amber had no need to think any further. In a flash she was reaching down the suit she had worn that day —no need to change her sweater. Quickly she donned her skirt and jacket, deciding to leave her flat-heeled shoes on since there probably wouldn't be any pavement until she reached the village. She topped her suit with her sheepskin jacket and listened at her door; all was silent. Opening her door, she saw from the faint glow coming up the stairs that the hall light had been left on, most likely for Mr Randle, she thought, and stealthily tiptoed down the stairs. She expelled a tense breath as she saw the front door had not been bolted— probably Mr Randle saw to that when he came in, passed through her mind; at least she didn't have to risk making a noise in drawing the bolts back.

Only when she was outside, the immense door to the house silently closed behind her, did she begin to breathe normally. But she had gone no more than a few yards, her sights set on turning right when she came to the end of the drive, when out of the eerie darkness a voice came to her and she nearly jumped out of her skin.

'If you're planning on doing a flit, you've forgotten your suitcase,' said Dyson Silver.

'You!' The word escaped Amber in a whisper, when she would much rather not have said anything.

'Yes, me. Having trouble in sleeping, Miss Newman? Don't tell me your guilty conscience is keeping you awake?' Amber wasn't planning on telling him anything. 'Or,' his voice hardened, 'have you come to meet your accomplice?'

'Accomplice?' she echoed.

'I'm sure you're batting those big brown eyes at me, but you're wasting your time, Miss Newman—even if I could see you, it wouldn't work.'

'Wouldn't work?' Amber pulled herself together; she was getting to sound like a poll parrot, repeating everything he said. 'I'm meeting no one,' she said more firmly than she felt, for he had the uncanniest knack of taking the ground right from under her. 'Did you think I'd come out here to tell my partner in crime where he could pick up the family jewels?' she jibed.

'No ... ?' he queried, though she hardly believed he was giving her the benefit of the doubt; he had already made up his mind she was an out-and-out bad lot. 'It's a cold night, Miss Newman.' He flicked on a torch she hadn't know he was carrying, and she screwed up her eyes as the beam from it hit her fully in the face, then moved away to carry on over her. 'You're dressed for the weather, I'll give you that, but if you haven't come creeping out of the house to meet someone—— Would I be asking too much, do you think, if I asked for an explanation?'

She read that he wasn't going to believe her whatever she said, and wished she had his gift for cutting sarcasm. He had switched the torch off now, thank goodness, but not before she had seen he too was wearing a sheepskin coat. Had he suspected she would come tip-toeing out from the front door? Had he been lying in wait for her? The thought displeased her that she was far from a trusted guest in his house, until the unwanted thought intruded that knowing what he personally knew of her—none of it good—it would be a bit much to expect him to take on trust anything Helen could have said to the good about her, when he knew her more intimately. That thought in itself made her bite her lip, and the husky note that penetrated her voice whenever she was disturbed was in evidence when she said:

'I know it looks bad from your point of view, Mr Silver,' she just couldn't call him Dyson, not with all the animosity she could feel coming from him, 'but the only reason for my creeping out of the house was that I didn't want to disturb anyone.'

'Exactly.'

She felt a spurt of temper at that, but quietened it. Time was getting on, she didn't have time to stop and argue with him if she was to be in church on time.

'Well, are you going to tell me what you're up to, or do we stand here all night? Whoever you've come to meet will be aware by now that your plans have fallen through.'

He would make her stand there all night too, she fumed—she had gathered that much about him. 'I haven't come to meet anyone,' she reiterated, then really exasperated, because she intended to keep faith with her mother and father regardless of anything he could think of to insult her with, 'If you must know, I was on my way to church.' There, she had told him, and if he was going to be sarcastic about that too, she would grab that torch out of his hand and wipe the sneering sarcasm off his face with it.

'Church?' he replied, his tone disbelieving.

'Yes, church,' she repeated, 'and if I don't go now I'm going to be too late.'

'You know where it is?'

'Helen told me it's just off the main road.'

There was silence for a few seconds, and Amber wondered if he was now ready to let her go. 'Why the sudden urge to go to church?' he asked, as she began to edge past him.

'I always go on Christmas Eve,' she said, and found herself adding, 'It's a—a—family thing.' Then because it was important to her and she knew she was going to be late if she didn't get a move on, 'Please, Dyson,' she said, her voice sounding choky. 'Please let me go.'

For long moments he didn't move. Then, 'I'll do more than that,' he said. 'I'll take you there myself.'

'You!' she exclaimed, unable to comprehend this about-face.

She waited for his acid reply to come, but there was none when he said, 'Yes, me. Did you think I wouldn't know where the church was?' and without waiting for her reply, 'Hang on here—I'll bring the car round.'

Not having wanted to go with him, Amber had to own she was glad he had decided to accompany her. For 'just off the main road' was nowhere near an adequate direction of how to get there, she saw, as he steered the car along the darkened main road, turned off and up a country lane, then took several more turns before pulling up a little way from the village church.

'I know,' he said, as they neared the illuminated entrance of the church and he could see from her expression that she was going to thank him for getting her there. 'Your Girl Guide instinct wouldn't have done you very much good, would it?'

'No,' Amber agreed, not questioning now the change in him, only too thankful that he was forgetting to bait her for a while as she walked with him a little way down the aisle where he found an empty pew, the front ones being already taken.

Amber was soon lost in the service and sang quietly alongside Dyson, who didn't have a bad voice himself, then forgot about him completely as she closed her eyes in prayer, her thoughts and prayers for her parents.

When they came out, she felt a calmness over her that had been missing whenever Dyson was anywhere in evidence. She saw him acknowledge several people, but he did not linger to speak with any of them, and this bore out an impression she had that he was a man who liked to keep himself to himself. She walked with him to his car, neither of them saying anything, then he was opening the door to the passenger side, telling her to, 'Get in—I won't be a moment,' before disappearing from her sight.

He wasn't gone long, and in his absence Amber took pleasure in watching others of the congregation, some talking in small groups, others hurrying on their way. The door to the driver's side opened and a cold blast of icy air came in with Dyson, though the ice she was getting used to from him was missing as to her surprise he apologised for keeping her waiting and pulled away from the kerb.

'Arthur's car sometimes plays him up. I went to check if he wanted a lift back, but he's had the trouble fixed.'

'Was Arthur the white-haired man at the end of the second row of the choir?' Amber asked, accepting that

Dyson's milk of human kindness extended to his house-keeper's husband but not to his house guest, before she caught herself up short to realise she would never have found the church in time if he hadn't offered to take her. She ignored the voice that said he had only taken her to church to call her bluff—she had enjoyed the service, and since the minister had spoken about human charity at this Christmastide, decided to look on him in that light as she heard him confirm that she had accurately picked out Arthur Randle.

Her feeling of goodwill to all men was still with her when Dyson brought the car to a standstill outside the front door of Moor View, saying, 'You go in—I'll put the car away.'

Her hand on the door handle, Amber half turned back to him. 'Thank you for taking me—I should have been too late if I'd tried to find the church on my own.' She thought she might be inviting an acid comment, but her thanks to him were due.

'Always glad to oblige,' he said, and she could make nothing from the way he said it how to take his words, though she was getting used to the two-edged way he had of speaking. She opened the car door and left him.

CHAPTER FIVE

AMBER was awakened on Christmas morning by Helen bringing in a tray bearing two cups of tea. Helen was in her dressing gown and explained as Amber struggled to sit up and banish sleep, 'Maureen was just coming up with your tea, so I thought I'd have mine with you. I can never lie in bed on Christmas morning,' she confessed, sending Amber an infectious grin. 'I'm like a big kid—I've already opened all my presents.' She dipped her hand into the pocket of her dressing gown and pulled out a small package gaily wrapped in Christmas paper. 'For you from me,' she smiled, dropping the gift in Amber's hands.

'I've got a present for you too,' said Amber, hopping out of bed and fetching it from the bottom of the wardrobe. She was still undecided what to do about the gifts she had for Dyson and Simon, and hadn't unpacked them from her case.

'Oh, good!' Helen exclaimed, and they both excitedly began to unwrap each other's present.

'Oh, Helen, it's beautiful,' Amber said softly, finding Helen had bought her a delicate gold chain. She knew it was expensive and was a little overcome that her friend couldn't have bought her anything she appreciated more—but it made her gift to Helen seem particularly unexciting by comparison.

'Super!' exclaimed Helen, when she opened the package Amber had given her. 'Thanks a lot,' and she lost no time in spraying some of the perfume on to her wrist. She insisted on giving Amber a squirt, regardless of the fact that they would both be bathing soon and washing it off. Helen then saw Amber was struggling with the unfamiliar clasp of the gold chain as she attempted to do it up around her throat. 'Here, let me,' she offered, then both girls were momentarily still as Dyson's voice sounded at the open doorway.

'Santa's been, then,' he said, coming into the room, his eyes surveying Amber in her shortie nightie, the gold chain about her throat. Amber coloured, more from being caught out of bed in her respectable but utterly feminine nightie, and her colour deepened as she saw his speculative gaze on her throat.

'Oh, Dyson, you're an angel!' Helen's squeal of delight took Dyson's eyes away from Amber, as Helen went and hugged him for his gift.

Amber took this opportunity to hurriedly take her dressing gown from the wardrobe and shrug into it. She hadn't liked at all that shrewd summing-up look he had given her, a look she read as saying she was only being friends with Helen for what she could get out of her—it made her feel sick.

She turned her thoughts away from her own feelings as Helen, still in the seventh heaven over Dyson's gift, was telling her he had bought her a fur coat. 'I gave out numerous hints starting months ago, but he never by so much as a flicker of an eye gave a sign that they'd penetrated.' She went on to say it wasn't an animal fur coat because she couldn't bear the thought of animals being slaughtered to cover her back. 'But it's a superb man-made imitation, it must have cost twice as much,' she said, enthralled.

'I saw it on a marked-down rack,' said Dyson, but nobody believed him. His nose twitched, and his glance went to the bottle of his stepsister's favourite perfume lying on the bed. 'This room smells like a . . .'

'Dyson!' Helen warned. 'Remember Amber's not used to your descriptive language.'

Not much she wasn't, Amber thought, meeting Dyson's eyes from where she sat on the edge of her bed and now swathed in her concealing dressing gown; she wouldn't forget in a hurry any of the names he had called her yesterday. There was nothing of the summing-up look in his face now as he extended his smile to her. 'I was merely going to say it smells like a—a lady's boudoir,' he lied smoothly. Then stretching out a hand to a parcel on the dressing table Amber was certain hadn't been there before he had come into the room, he picked it up and handed it to her. 'Merry Christmas, Amber,' he said, and there was none of the sarcasm she had expected to hear in his voice. Obviously she thought, because Helen was present.

'Hurry up and open it,' Helen urged, getting more enjoyment from anticipating what was inside than Amber was.

Slowly Amber undid the wrapping, hoping with all her heart that it was a proper gift and not some cynical reminder of what lay between them.

'Oh!' she exclaimed, shock hitting her as, the wrapper off, she gazed in wonder at Dyson's gift to her.

'Helen said you were a romantic,' said Dyson, seeming to observe that his gift of an expensively bound volume of *Jane Eyre* had taken her breath away.

Amber had no idea what she had let slip for Helen to have gained the impression she was a romantic, but she was so right, and had the present been from anyone but Dyson, she knew she would have treasured it all her life.

'It—it's lovely,' she said huskily. 'Th-thank you, Dyson.' Now was the time to present him with the tie she had bought for him, but she was too shaken to move, then Helen was saying:

'Aren't you going to give him a kiss for it?—it is Christmas, after all!'

Amber's eyes winged in his direction. She knew he didn't want her to kiss him, any more than she wanted to kiss him, then mercifully as those hard eyes looked steadily back at her, she was saved from having to do anything, for Simon was in the room.

'What's all this about kissing?' he asked, and where Dyson was dressed in slacks and a sweater, Simon was still in pyjamas and dressing gown, the mussed-up state of his hair telling them all he had just got out of bed.

'Dyson has just given Amber her Christmas present— I was suggesting she showed her thanks by giving him a kiss,' Helen informed him.

'Damn,' muttered Simon, embarrassed. 'I didn't get you a present, Amber.'

'Which leaves us wondering whether you're sorry you didn't get Amber a present—or if you're sorry you're not going to get to kiss her,' Dyson inserted.

'There's mistletoe downstairs,' Simon replied, recovering quickly.

Dyson's tones were cool when he remarked, 'It's getting to be like a fairground in here,' and walked out.

The moment had gone when Amber could have given Dyson the present she had for him, and in view of Simon's embarrassment that he had nothing for her, she didn't think she could give him his present now and risk causing him further embarrassment. And really, she thought, when once again she had her room to herself, she could hardly give Dyson something and leave Simon out. Oh well, Uncle James would have a bonus Christmas gift when she got back.

After breakfast, Helen took her and showed her round outside the house, and in the beauty of the view before her, for Moor View was exactly what its name implied and had an uninterrupted view of rolling hills and moorland, Amber forgot that the brief respite from

Dyson's cynicism when he had taken her to church last night was over, and she gazed in delight at the view.

'Come and see the stables.' Helen was used to the view and now took it for granted, though Amber thought if she was lucky enough to live in such a delightful spot, never would she ever tire of such wild beauty. But she went uncomplaining with Helen to the stables at the rear of the house. She had had riding lessons when she had been at school, and had enjoyed them, she loved horses too, but knew she would never do more than be able to adequately acquit herself. Brilliant horsewoman she was not, but the sight of the grey gelding which Helen said she rode more than any of the others was such a magnificent specimen, she was pulled with the sudden urge to be up astride and galloping into those rolling hills she had for the moment been forced to turn her back on.

'Beautiful, isn't he?' Helen asked, though no reply was necessary, for Starlight had completely won Amber's sigh of admiration. 'Do you ride?' Helen enquired.

'I haven't for ages.'

'How do you fancy coming for a ride tomorrow? It's too late now, and we're going to be too full after lunch today to want to move—but we could take a couple of horses out tomorrow. I expect Simon will come with us without us having to ask.'

'Do you mind if I don't?' Amber felt terrible at having to refuse Helen's kind offer, but although apart from that twinge in her back when Dyson had tossed her carelessly on the bed she had been pain-free, she wasn't sure her back was up to the rough treatment it would encounter bumping up and down on the back of a horse.

She was glad to see Helen wasn't put out by her refusal. 'See how you feel about it tomorrow,' she suggested. 'If you haven't been on top of a horse for some time they can seem as high as a house!'

They left it there, with Amber saying she would think about it, though her mind was already made up—much as she would have loved to go with Helen and Simon, she didn't see how she could; it would be asking for trouble.

As Helen's remark had indicated, lunch was a filling meal, starting off with asparagus soup, through to turkey, chestnut stuffing, minute sausages, bacon rolls, braised celery, potatoes and sprouts, so that as they had a breather while waiting for the Christmas pudding, they each without exception said they would only want the smallest portion. A different wine had been served with each course, and Amber's cheeks had two spots of pink in them, for all she had refused to have more than one glass of each offering.

Dyson was being nicer to her than he had previously shown, and a pleasurable feeling of being able to relax with him came over her for the first time as Helen and Simon's banter flowed freely, and she laughed quite naturally at some of the wit that went to and fro.

'It's all right for you,' said Simon, as the talk got round to some of his exploits at university. 'You're only playing at that tuppeny-ha'penny job you got for yourself, Helen. You know you can pack it in any time you want, but if I don't want Dyson here to separate me from my breath, I've got to slog on.'

'Ah, diddums,' Helen said unsympathetically. 'I've seen you students on television—the great unwashed ...'

'You haven't got a clue what it's all about, have you?' Simon fired up suddenly.

Amber was suddenly wary that she was going to witness at first hand a family squabble, not between Dyson and Simon as she had been told by Helen would happen if she wasn't there, but between Helen herself and Simon. Her stomach churned over, the relaxed feeling left her, but only for a moment, for she caught the warning look Dyson gave Simon, a speaking look that clearly said, 'Remember your manners—we have a guest.'

Simon's glance went from his brother to Amber. 'Sorry,' he smiled engagingly. 'I'm working on my thesis at the moment—I guess I had an attack of sour grapes at missing where it's all at.'

Amber smiled in return, her stomach back to normal, the relaxed feeling returning as she questioned Simon about his thesis.

'It's all done bar the shouting—now if I could find some pretty little typist to type it for me ...'

'I'll type it for you if you like,' Amber instantly volunteered, relieved that she wasn't going to witness a family fight, and speaking without thought.

'You type, Amber?' this from Dyson, and Amber realised while Simon thought she, like Helen, was holding down a tuppeny-ha'penny job, as a typist she had a skill at her fingertips. The humour of that thought struck her—fingertips, typing, she thought, and barely covered the fact that she was holding back a laugh as she glanced at Dyson sitting next to her.

'Oh yes,' she confirmed, then because, ridiculously, she still wanted to laugh and needed to say something to get her over it, 'I'm a trained secretary.'

'What the dickens is a trained secretary doing working for peanuts at Brewsters?' Simon broke in.

Amber didn't feel like laughing any longer, as it dawned on her she had been talking too freely. Simon's question had been a natural one, but she couldn't answer him, not then, as remembrance stormed in of the

real reason she had given up her job—Mr Turner, she
knew, would have kept her job open for her until her
injuries had healed. She found Dyson's eyes on her, he
seemed as interested as Simon in her answer, and she
couldn't help wondering how Dyson would react if she
said she was no longer working as a secretary because
she had thought she was going to be the mother of his
child.

A hot blush stained her cheeks as she turned her eyes
away from him. She knew she was looking guilty, knew
they were all looking at her, was aware of Dyson's enquiring look in particular, and said lamely, 'I thought
I'd like a change.'

'Where were you working before you went to Brewsters?' Simon asked, but Helen cut him off as though
sensing that Amber was feeling uncomfortable.

'Mind your own business,' she said a shade sharply,
and Amber, thinking there was the makings of that
family squabble yet from the way Helen spoke, forced
a light laugh.

'It's no state secret, Helen—I worked for a firm of
solicitors.'

'I don't blame you for packing it in, then,' said
Simon, apparently not in any way upset by his sister's
brisk admonishment. 'I can't imagine anything more
deadly dull than working in a solicitors office.'

No one heard as the Christmas pudding was brought
in aflame, Dyson's murmured aside to Amber, 'Not unless it's working for Brewsters.' Amber flicked him a
hasty glance, but he was not looking at her, but replen-
ishing Helen's glass.

After the meal they watched the Queen's speech on
television, then Simon said he would be nodding off if
he didn't get some exercise. 'Who's coming for a walk?'

'Coming, Amber?' Helen asked, rising to her feet

with a groan. 'I shan't be able to eat any tea if I don't walk this lot off, and Mrs Randle's Christmas cake is not to be missed.' Amber was ready to get her coat when Helen asked, 'What about you, Dyson—are you coming?'

'I have some papers I want to look through,' he replied.

'Oh, Dyson, not on Christmas Day!' wailed Helen, and Amber didn't hear what he said to that as she made for the door intending to go and collect her coat, but heard Helen come back, 'I know time and tide wait for no man, but really, Dyson . . .'

The start of their walk was not begun very enthusiastically, and strangely, where she would have thought she was glad Dyson was not with them, Amber found herself missing his presence. How odd, she mused, before putting the strange notion out of her head and blaming it on to the wine she had consumed.

On their return an hour later, Amber was glad she had made the effort. For all the wind was cold, she no longer felt sluggish, and as Helen and Simon had broken into witty banter from time to time, they had laughed often, and she was able to forget the peculiar notion that she had wanted Dyson to come with them.

'I'll go and rustle up a cup of tea,' Helen told them as they went through the front door, and left Amber with Simon as they went towards the staircase.

'Just a minute.'

Simon's voice halted her as she had one foot on the first stair. She looked at him questioningly, a smile of enquiry on her lips, then saw his glance go up above her head. Her eyes followed his, and she saw a sprig of mistletoe had been suspended from the chandelier.

'Oh, Simon,' she said helplessly, and went to continue her way upstairs, not thinking he was serious.

'Not so fast,' she heard him say, and felt a terrific pain in her lower spine as he pulled her backwards, twisting her round. Then he was kissing her, but she was more aware of the pain than of the pleasure his lips were seeking. She put up her hands to push him away, knew she was badly off balance and as he pulled his mouth away from hers she had to cling on to him as another spear of pain darted through her, causing her to close her eyes while it washed over her.

When she opened her eyes, she was aghast to see Dyson had come out of his study and was looking at her with a look of icy contempt. He then turned smartly away and disappeared out of her view. She heard a door slam, and didn't need any help in guessing he was giving vent to his anger by misusing the door.

'More?' questioned Simon, realising she was making no effort to get away from him.

'Er . . .' Amber came back to the fact that Simon still had his arms about her. 'I don't think so, Simon,' she forced a smile. 'That kiss will last me a long while.' She eased herself out of his arms and he reluctantly let her go.

'I shall stand here in wait,' he was threatening as she went upstairs to shed her coat.

Amber sat down as soon as she gained her room. She had pain-killers in her suitcase—she had popped them in as a precaution, but hadn't really thought she would need them. Perhaps the pain would soon go off; she had had twinges before and they hadn't lasted long. Deciding against taking any tablets, she left her chair and went to hang up her coat. She would have to go down; they had all said they were gasping for a cup of tea when Moor View had come into sight, and it would look more than odd if she didn't join Helen and Simon, and she didn't want Helen sending Maureen up with a cup—Maureen had had enough to do in helping with the lunch; she was probably enjoying a well earned rest.

After washing her hands and face, Amber cleaned her teeth which felt all furry from the wine she had had, and left her room knowing any relaxing in Dyson's attitude towards her would be gone the next time she saw him. Hadn't he warned her not to try any of her little games with his brother? And she couldn't very well go up to him and say, look, Simon made a grab for me, I couldn't do anything about it. He wouldn't believe her anyway.

She was about three steps down from the bottom when she heard footsteps coming along the hall. Remembering what Simon had said about lying in wait for her, even though she didn't believe it, she faltered as she waited away from the mistletoe to see who it was.

Her heart sank as Dyson came into view. Simon she could cope with, but Dyson, a Dyson still with that cold look of contempt for her on his face, was something entirely different.

'Well, if it isn't the little bar-hop,' he drawled insultingly, and Amber experienced again the same feeling of nausea that gripped her every time it came to her that she could not defend herself because what he was saying had been true.

She would dearly have loved to turn away from him and retrace her steps back to her room, but stubborn courage took possession of her and she forced herself to descend the three remaining stairs until she was on a level with him. She had nothing she wanted to say to him, and fully expected him to move out of her way, but he didn't. She made to go round him, but felt her arm caught in a hold it was impossible to break from if she wanted to keep her dignity.

'I thought I told you to keep out of Simon's way,' he said coldly.

'No,' Amber replied slowly, a spurt of anger coming from somewhere making it easier to stand up to him, 'you didn't say that—as I remember it you told me to keep out of his bedroom while I was here.' She had to look at him to see how he was taking that she wasn't scuttling away under his freezingly cold contempt. She saw from the way his eyes had narrowed that he wasn't liking it at all, and where his look should have silenced her, it only served to spur her on. 'Since you're so concerned about your brother's moral welfare, perhaps I should tell you I haven't made it to his bedroom,' she paused, then added, her voice deliberately provocative, 'yet.'

She knew as that word floated between them she had gone too far. In her opinion Simon was more able to take care of himself than she was, but it was obvious Dyson didn't think so, for the icy contempt he had been regarding her with disappeared, and a look of pure fury burned in his face and she felt his other hand take hold of her and he swung her round, jarring her back so that she winced.

He mistook the wince of pain that crossed her face for a spasm of fear, and hauled her close up against his muscular body. Amber couldn't remember being this close to him before and struggled to get away as real fear hit her.

'Yes, you can look frightened,' he gritted in her ear. 'I'm telling you now, you little trollop—keep away from Simon, or I'll make it so difficult for you you'll never be allowed into a decent home again.'

'Decent home?' Amber echoed. Where did he think she had come from if it wasn't a decent home? And as that thought was followed by the realisation that what he was saying was an insult to her dead parents, a fury not to be denied stormed through her, and since once again the hold he had on her prevented her from using her arms and hands, she drew back her foot and aimed a kick at the leg she knew must still be bruised from her last assault on him.

He let out an oath as her foot connected with his shin, and a fury came over him that transcended anything that had gone before, and though he must have been in agony, he refused to let her go as the grip on her arms tightened, so that it was she who cried out in pain, not him.

'You're hurting me!' she moaned.

'I'm glad, you little vixen!' His head thrust forward aggressively, and she thought he was going to murder her, until his head, inches away from her, the awful feeling came to her that no, he wasn't going to hit her or kill her, he was going to kiss her.

In sheer and utter panic she tore her right hand away, and although he still had hold of her arm she was able to place her hand in front of his mouth.

'No,' she whispered hoarsely, 'don't kiss me.'

'Kiss you?' Dyson repeated, as though that was the last thing he had in mind, only she was too panic-stricken to notice. His eyes suddenly became thoughtful as it looked as though she was more terror-stricken that he should kiss her than give her the beating she so richly deserved. A gleam lit his eyes that could only be described as devilish. 'Why, when you're so free with your—favours—should you be terrified at the most unlikely thought that I should want to kiss you?' he asked softly.

Some of Amber's panic subsided, but she was still too strung up to invent anything; her terror had been very real.

'I . . . I d-don't want to re-remember,' she said huskily.

'Remember?' he questioned. 'What is it you don't want to remember, my dear Miss Nymphomaniac Newman?'

Amber kept her hand in front of his mouth—she was sure he had kissed her before. Or had he taken her without leading up to it at all? Was that what had caused her amnesia about that night? Had his love-making been that of an animal? She just didn't know—all she knew was that she was glad of the blackness in her mind and couldn't risk him kissing her and bringing her memory to life.

'Please,' she choked as he took her hand away. 'Please don't kiss me!'

'Do you think your second attempt to put me on crutches should go unrewarded?' he asked softly, and Amber didn't trust the softness of his tones. 'Something about my kissing you frightens you, doesn't it, Miss Butter-wouldn't-melt-Newman? Well, I think it's high time you had something to be afraid of—— Who knows, it might even put an end to your promiscuity?'

'No—oh no!' Amber felt terror rush through her again as Dyson pinned both hands behind her back with one hand and held her chin firmly with the other. Her blinding terror left her defenceless, she didn't even have the strength to kick out at him. Then his head was coming nearer, the distance from his mouth to hers lessening. 'Please don't do this, Dyson,' she begged, then her lips were silenced, her words lost in her throat as his mouth came down over hers.

Almost fainting, she waited for the unwanted remembrances of that night to come storming in and tear her apart—but nothing happened. She felt Dyson's lips against her own—not harsh and cruel as she had expected, but gentle and persuasive, as if at the very last moment he had realised she was almost fainting with terror and had changed his mind about inflicting further punishment on her.

She made no move to respond, but stood stiffly as he

let go the hold he had over her wrists and put that arm around her. Then he pulled back his head, looking deeply into her eyes as though puzzled by her lack of response.

Had she responded without reserve that other time? Amber wondered as she gazed back at him. Then Dyson's eyes hardened at the innocent look of her, and he brought his head down again, and this time there was nothing gentle in his kiss as he forced her lips apart and held her with both arms around her. Amber felt a flickering spark of response within her as he pressed her body up against him, she could feel his thighs pressing into her, wanted to press herself against him of her own volition, then as his one hand left the small of her back and settled insinuatingly on her hip, she realised if she responded to him now it would only endorse what he already knew from her one lapse, that she was easy. Her hand went down to rest on his at her hip and she pulled it back to her waist, surprise catching her that he allowed her to do so.

His head pulled back from her and for speechless seconds they looked at each other. 'You kiss like a virgin,' seemed to be dragged from him.

The sound of his voice in the mesmerised world she found herself in had realisation rushing in, that after that first gentle kiss she had no longer struggled to get away from him. The terrible realisation that she had wanted this man who thought she was of no account to go on kissing her, had wanted to respond, and only the thought that she wouldn't earn his respect that way had stopped her.

It was that last thought that had her saying, 'Well, you know for sure I'm not a virgin, don't you?' She wished she could have held his eyes then, but she couldn't. She looked down at his dark-shirted chest, and heard that the hardness had returned to his voice.

'I do indeed,' he gritted, and dropped his arms away from her.

'There you are.' Helen's voice broke in as Amber was searching for something to say while knowing there was no answer to what Dyson had said. 'What are you two doing there?' She came up to them, her voice slightly puzzled at seeing her friend and her step-brother standing so close to each other yet not saying a word. 'Oh, you've been taking advantage of the mistle-toe,' she smiled as light suddenly dawned, and seemed pleased that the two of them were getting on so well to-gether.

'Something like that,' Dyson admitted, and gave Amber a deprecating look Helen couldn't see, before turning without another word and going into his study.

No one seemed particularly hungry at dinner that night. 'Not surprising,' Helen commented, 'considering what we put away at lunch time.'

For her part, every mouthful Amber ate felt like chaff in her mouth. Perhaps she would have fared better if Dyson had decided not to join them at the table—It was hoping for too much, she sighed inwardly, to hope he would get lost in his papers and decide to have his dinner in his study, for all he wasn't eating very much either. She caught his glance on her, and not liking his superior look she turned her eyes away. Oh, why did he have to plague her with his presence? Even if it was his house and she was only here at his insis-tence, she knew he had only deigned to grace the table eating a meal he obviously didn't want, purely to see what she got up to with Simon. Sitting there like some avenging spirit—what did he think she was going to do, for goodness' sake—strip off and chase Simon to his room?

'... with me?' Amber, lost in her thoughts of wishing

she could make an effigy of Dyson and spend the night sticking pins into it, came to to hear Simon addressing her.

'I'm sorry, Simon,' she said smiling pleasantly, because he had no part in the battle that raged between her and Dyson whenever they were alone together for two minutes at a time.

'I was saying I've been invited to a party tonight—I was asking if you would like to come with me?'

Anything was better than staying here with Dyson sending her his holier-than-thou looks for the rest of the evening. Amber opened her mouth to say she would love to go, then for some unknown reason she flicked a glance in Dyson's direction and what she saw there had her rapidly changing her mind. For his look clearly said, you go anywhere with Simon and I'll be waiting for you when you get back—you won't escape me if I have to wait in your room to sort you out.

'Er—I don't think so, Simon,' she said, trying to make her voice sound casual. 'We were up early this morning and I—er—like to go to bed early.' She wished she hadn't glanced at Dyson again, his look plainly said, 'I'll bet!'

Simon didn't take her refusal very gracefully, but Helen saying she thought she would have an early night too made Amber's excuse more plausible.

When Simon had left for his party Dyson once more disappeared to his study. Had to wait in case I changed my mind, Amber thought mutinously, but she was glad he didn't sit with her and Helen while they watched an hour of television. Her back wasn't feeling any too easy and she didn't want Helen thinking she was somebody's granny if she stuffed a cushion behind her to support it, so waiting for a break in the programmes, when the ormolu clock on the mantelpiece said ten o'clock, she got to her feet.

'Do you mind if I go up, Helen?'

'Not at all—shan't be long behind you myself.'

Wasn't it just her luck, Amber fumed, to leave the sitting room just as Dyson was leaving his study! Well, luck was partly with her, she thought, as she decided she wouldn't give him the chance to ignore her, and went to sail past him with her chin held high. At least she had got out of the sitting room before he had decided to come and join them.

'Did you remember?' Dyson's cynical tones stopped her before she had gone more than two steps past him.

'Sorry—I'm not with you?'

'I was asking if my kissing you had made you remember whatever it was you were trying to forget? It was obviously something only I could trigger off.'

He was too clever by far, Amber thought. Not only that, but he had had moments alone in his study to consider everything that had taken place—trust him to sum up that she had shown no terror while in Simon's arms, so it therefore followed as he had so shrewdly surmised, that it was only his kiss she was afraid of.

'Oh, that,' she shrugged, her tones as offhand as his were cynical. 'One always tries to forget something unpleasant.'

She saw his eyes were watching her intently, her jibe sailing infuriatingly over his head.

'Well, at least you learned something from experience,' he said obliquely.

'Oh?' He couldn't know that her memory of that night was still as blank as ever.

'You refused Simon's invitation to go with him to the party,' he enlightened her.

'You can't be there to watch him all the time,' she came back, thinking her retort was rather good since there was no knowing what she and Simon would get up to when he wasn't watching. She turned to go, thinking she had had the last word, and heard him reminding her, his voice dripping with unpleasantness:

'It's not Simon I'm watching—I'm keeping my eyes on every move you make, Miss Newman.'

CHAPTER SIX

AMBER reached her room to sit down heavily on the small bedroom chair. She held her hands out in front of her, saw their evidence that she was shaking. Oh, was there ever such a vile man—— Why did it have to be him she had picked on that night? There couldn't be many men as cynical, as horrible as him. And she was stuck here at Moor View—even if she could get some mode of transport to take her home, she was held here by the friendship she enjoyed with Helen. She could never tell Helen the full story—couldn't tell anyone—besides which, Helen had intimated that Dyson and Simon would be at each other's throats the minute she left the house.

With a resigned thought that this was perhaps her punishment for her sins, she carefully undressed and climbed into bed. Her pain-killers were still in her case, but it seemed too much of an effort to get out of bed and take a couple. Which just went to prove, she thought, that the pain wasn't as bad as she thought it was.

It was around two o'clock in the morning when she woke up covered in perspiration. Quickly she reached and turned on the light, glad to see she was still in the same room in which she had dropped off to sleep. Her nightmare had been very real. She had been back in North Wales again, trying to get to her parents, trying to claw her way out from the rock fall. It was not a new dream, but it was so long since she had had it she knew it must have been instigated by the pain she had experienced when getting ready for bed. She moved again, recalled that she had felt no discomfort when moving to switch on the light, and knew that all that had been needed for the pain to go was for her to lie down and rest her body. That in itself was a relief. Uncle James had been right in saying she would heal before the year was out if she took care. She turned off her light, then sat up and turned it on again. It was no good, her nightmare was too real, too near to be banished quickly. The darkness had her remembering every detail. There was no one to see if she slept with the light on and if she didn't wake before Maureen arrived with her tea in the morning, she could pretend she had been reading and had dropped off. Amber reached across to the bedside table and picked up the paperback she had unpacked on Christmas Eve but had so far not looked at. She let it drop gently to the floor as evidence, not wanting anyone to know of her weakness in sleeping with the light on.

She was still wide awake when a faint tapping at her door startled her. She was even more startled when Simon, a slightly merry Simon, came into her room.

'Saw your light from under the door,' he said, laughing lightly. 'Was it meant to be a guiding light, Amber?' Something in what he said made him laugh again, but Amber couldn't see anything very funny.

'How many have you had?' she asked him, not wishing to be unpleasant, but not liking to have him in her room in this state.

'Only a few—only a few,' he protested. 'There wasn't a girl to touch you for looks at the party, Amber. Why didn't you come with me?'

'I told you, I was tired.'

'But you're still awake.'

'I was asleep,' Amber lied pointedly, 'until you came in.'

'Asleep?' he scoffed, grinning glassy-eyed at her.

'What was your light doing on, then? Ha—got you there,' he said triumphantly, and nearly fell over.

Amber was torn between the desire to get up and frogmarch him out of her room, and the desire to giggle. Some men were funny when they were drunk.

'I'd been reading,' she said, glad that she'd thought to place her evidence on the floor. 'I must have dropped off.'

'Huh,' said Simon as though he didn't believe her.

'There's my book there,' Amber told him, pointing to it.

'Damn—I thought my luck had changed,' Simon sighed, and peering down to see where Amber had indicated, promptly did fall over.

'Shh—you'll wake the whole house!'

Simon laughed, not a bit bothered, then returned to renew his advances. 'I like you, Amber—I really, really like you.'

'And I like you, Simon,' Amber tried to go along so far. 'But I shan't like you very much if you don't leave me to go back to sleep. Go to your own room—please, Simon!'

'You don't want—a party?'

'No, Simon, I don't want a party.'

He staggered over to the door, and Amber felt relief rush in that he was at last going to go. She watched him as he turned at the door. He then seemed to make a definite effort to prove he could carry his liquor, squaring his shoulders as his hand found the door handle. He looked so ridiculous, Amber felt her giggles rising up inside her. 'Spoilsport,' he said, and opened the door and went through it. Amber almost choked on her desire to laugh.

In a way, although his intention to get her into bed with him if she would have allowed it was offensive, she wasn't sorry he had come in to see her. His visit had successfully pushed her nightmare into the background, and since her back no longer pained her, she thought what was left of the night could be spent in untroubled sleep. She leaned over and snicked out the light.

When she awakened, she was feeling less charitable towards Simon. Were both brothers tarred with the same brush? Dyson had said that she was hot for anything in trousers, but she was beginning to think both brothers were hot for anything that wore a skirt. She got up and bathed and dressed in jeans and a shirt. Helen had mentioned going riding, but Amber thought discretion would be the better part of valour—her back was all right again now, but she didn't think she had better risk it, irksome though it was. There would be other times when she could go riding if she so felt like doing. If both Helen and Simon were going riding, and no mention had been made of Dyson joining them, then she would take herself off for a walk. She had no wish to be left alone with Dyson, always supposing he didn't intend to shut himself in his study —she had no wish to be left alone with Simon either, come to that.

She met Helen, similarly dressed to herself, just going into the breakfast room. Helen smiled warmly as she pushed open the door, but Amber's answering smile faded as she saw Dyson was already seated at the table, the look in his eyes chilling. Well, she hadn't expected him to beam all over his face at her, had she? Though this was the first time he had shown himself less than pleasant to her with Helen present.

Helen was chatting naturally away as she helped herself and Amber from the warming tray, completely oblivious to any atmosphere between her stepbrother and her friend.

'Are you coming riding with us after all, Amber?'

she asked, tackling her breakfast with a healthy appetite. Amber didn't actually ask 'Us?' but it was there in her eyes; she definitely wasn't going riding if Dyson was going. 'Simon and me,' Helen enlightened her. 'If he ever decides to get up—he's a tired old thing.'

'Probably exhausted himself last night,' said Dyson, his eyes holding Amber's in a cold stare. She had an idea there was something more behind his comment than was obvious, but decided to ignore him, though she saw Helen give him a quick look as though she too suspected some hidden meaning.

'Well, he probably didn't come home till dawn, seeing that it was Kit Lancaster's party he went to.' She turned back to Amber, explaining, 'Kit's mother always gets lashings of bacon and eggs in when Kit throws a party just in case they all stay to breakfast.'

Amber could have told her that Simon hadn't stayed to breakfast, that it had still been dark when he had come home, but since Helen would no doubt feel terrible on her behalf if she made it known that Simon had made a detour to her room before he eventually made it to his bed, she refrained from saying anything.

She was just telling Helen she wouldn't be riding that morning and assuring her, in reply to Helen's question, that she didn't mind one bit if Helen went without her, when the door opened and Simon came in. He promptly sat down and reached for the cereals.

'Good morning, Simon,' Dyson said pointedly, and in reminding Simon that he had forgotten his manners, reminded Amber that she had given him no word of greeting either. She excused herself by thinking the way Dyson had looked at her he wouldn't have answered anyway.

'Good morning,' Simon said generally round the table, his eyes fixing on Amber, willing her to look at him. But Amber didn't want to talk to Simon either this morning, especially with Dyson watching so closely. She wasn't a sufficiently good actress for it not to show that she was upset with Simon, and she didn't want Dyson asking questions as to the reason.

'You look as though you had a heavy night,' Helen opined, when Simon refused her offer to get him some bacon and eggs.

'I'm sure he has,' Dyson put in coldly, and stood up, tossing his napkin on to the table. Then, looking glacially at his stepbrother, 'I'd like a word with you in my study when you're sufficiently back in the land of the living.' With that he favoured Amber with another chilling glance and strode from the room.

'What's bitten him?' Simon asked as soon as the door was closed.

'Haven't a clue,' Helen replied. 'Have you been up to anything, Simon?' Then, her voice sharpening, 'You haven't sold more ...'

'Of course I haven't—— Hell, d'you think I'm daft or something? I haven't forgotten the last ...' he broke off as he realised Amber was with them, and there was a tense pause while Amber wondered if she could leave her breakfast half way through and let brother and sister have their discussion in private. Then Simon seemed to recognise that she was feeling uncomfortable.

'Are you coming riding with us, Amber?' he asked. 'Please say yes.'

'No, I don't think so.' Amber flicked a glance at him and couldn't be at odds with him any longer. He had the air of a little boy who knew he had done something wrong and was at pains to make up for it. She smiled at him. 'I thought I would go for a nice long walk.'

Simon tried to get her to change her mind, but when he could see that she wouldn't, the subject was left and breakfast was finished with the three of them chatting about everything and anything.

Amber folded her napkin preparing to go upstairs for her jacket. 'Ready?' said Simon to Helen.

'Aren't you going to see Dyson first?' Helen asked.

'Like hell,' Simon replied. 'I want a clear head if I'm going to get chalked off about something—— If we look sharp we can shoot past the study and we'll be out on the moors before he knows we've gone.'

'Oh, Simon, do you think we should?' Helen looked hesitant.

'Oh, come on,' Simon urged. 'He can't hang us.' But he enlisted Amber's aid by asking her to stay in the breakfast room until she saw them pass the window, telling her that Dyson would think the three of them were still there until he heard the door close as she left the room.

Feeling very much a conspirator, Amber watched as they silently opened the door and crept along the hall. She saw them race past the breakfast-room window and out of sight, and thought to give them a few more minutes before going up to her room for her coat. Who did Dyson think he was anyway?

In all, she waited five minutes before she left the room, but didn't dare stay any longer in case Dyson became suspicious of the silence and came to investigate. The next time she saw him would be too soon. Hoping he would decide to have his lunch sent to him in his study but not holding out much hope of that, Amber left the breakfast room, closing the door firmly and doing nothing to deaden her footsteps. She was at the bottom of the staircase when her heart sank.

'I want a word with you.'

Dyson's cold tones addressed to her back had a shiver of fear running down her spine, before it came to her that she had done nothing wrong; it was Simon who was due for some of the carpet treatment, not her. She turned, her chin tilting up a few degrees.

'Me?' she queried, wishing he wasn't so tall and she could look down her nose at him. 'I thought it was Simon who was in your black books?'

'I'm quite well aware that by now Simon is out on the moors somewhere,' Dyson told her, his cold anger not abating at the arrogant stance she was taking with him. 'In my study, Miss Newman.'

Amber stood her ground. She had no idea how he knew Simon had sneaked out of the house rather than go and see him—perhaps Simon had done the same sort of thing before, she mused—but to say, 'In my study' as though she had no choice in the matter ... She turned her back on him and put a foot on the first stair.

'Very well, Miss Newman, we'll talk in your bedroom.' She heard his footsteps behind her and turned hurriedly, her eyes widening at the purposeful expression on his face. She sensed then that he was absolutely furious with her about something, and began to feel afraid again. 'I'm sure you're more at home in your bedroom—we'll talk there.' He was standing beside her, his hand beneath her elbow, urging her to go up the stairs with him.

Anger began to spark inside her, ousting her fear of him. She snatched her elbow out of his grasp and without a word turned and marched into his study.

She had never been in this room before, and she saw, while Dyson came in behind her closing the door with a decisive click, that his study too was a large room, oak-panelled, with a desk with businesslike impedimenta strewn liberally around, a well worn chair, pictures on the wall she had no time or interest in just then.

'Sit down, Miss Newman.'

'I'm not staying that long.'

'Sit down!' he barked, and almost pushed her to sit on the leather-upholstered settee to the side of her.

'There's no need to manhandle me,' she objected, furious to find herself seated when it hadn't been her intention to do so.

'I should think one more dose of manhandling was neither here nor there where you're concerned,' he said nastily.

Amber bit her lip. What defence had she got against that? 'You know everything,' she said, unable to sit quiet without making some sort of retort to let him know she wasn't to be cowed by him.

'Yes, I do, don't I,' he agreed. 'Though I'm sure you'd much rather I didn't.' This time Amber did keep quiet. 'I thank God for that night last September when you left me in no doubt how free with your favours you really are. Had it not been for that night, I might well have been taken in by the demure attitude you've adopted since coming here as Helen's friend.'

'Surely not?' Amber jibed. 'Surely no one could put anything over on the great Mr Dyson Silver?'

He ignored her jibe. 'I bet you thought it was Christmas and birthday time all rolled into one when Helen invited you here and you learned that not only did she have two unattached brothers, but found out from *Uncle James* that the family were "well-to-do". What was in your mind, dear Miss not-so-demure Newman? Did you think to get your hooks into one or other of us?'

'Hooks?' Amber picked on that one word, when she wanted to scream and shout at him, defend Uncle James to the last ditch.

'Marriage, Miss Newman—marriage.'

'Marriage?' she questioned. Then as what he was really saying hit her, 'I wouldn't marry either of you if you were the last men breathing!' she stormed, and attempted to get up, then was angrier than ever that he was standing over her blocking her way.

'You won't get the chance,' he bit back at her. 'Why should either of us marry you—even supposing there was the remotest possibility of that—when we can both have *everything* you have to offer without the need of a preacher?'

Amber felt a familiar nausea hit her at his words, but she managed to control it—she wasn't going out of this room with her tail between her legs, that was for sure.

'Both of you?' she said sarcastically.

'Both of us,' he reiterated, some of his coldness leaving him as a fury she didn't care for lit his eyes. 'You really burned your boats when you allowed Simon into your room last night. If marriage to you ever entered his head before you so happily welcomed him, he's not likely to want to marry you, since you "offer yourself for free".'

Vaguely Amber recalled his saying something similar on that night last September, but she was more concerned now with the fact that he knew somehow or other that Simon had come to her room in the early hours of this morning. She saw clearly that Dyson wasn't going to believe her about last night whatever she told him, and it was sheer bravado, nothing more, that had her answering:

'What's the matter, Dyson? Crabby because it wasn't you I welcomed?'

She heard his sharply indrawn breath, and looked up to see the fury she had seen in his eyes had turned into molten metal, and she knew she had overstepped the mark as fierce hands came down and gripped her in a bone-crushing hold.

'No, damn you—I could have you any time I wanted —and you know it!'

'You couldn't,' she denied hotly, all pretence at being a woman who knew all the answers vanishing fast as she experienced the same terror she had yesterday when she had thought he was going to kiss her. There seemed to be a threat in his words, and she knew if he forced himself on her again, this time there would be no holding her memory at bay—for her own peace of mind that memory had to stay blank.

Too late she saw Dyson's eyes narrow and realised he had seen her terror, seen it and slotted it into the correct pigeonhole. With his hands still on her shoulders he sat down on the settee beside her, turning her to face him.

'I told you to keep out of Simon's way or I'd make sure you were never allowed into a decent home again,' he told her, his mouth a hard line. 'I can see now that that threat hasn't worried you at all, but you've just given me an idea for a far more fitting punishment.'

With sickening dread Amber knew what he had in mind. 'No,' she whispered hoarsely. 'No, don't!'

'Oh, but yes,' Dyson said menacingly. 'I may not like having to soil myself by touching you—but for such a loose-moralled hussy, the idea of me in particular touching you fills you with terror, doesn't it?'

'Please don't,' Amber begged, and saw, her fear growing, that he was too angry to listen to her pleas.

'Do you know what I'm going to do, Miss Newman?' he said, savouring every moment of her fear of him. 'I'm going to make love to you—though it will hardly be love—more slow, deliberate sex.'

'You can't,' she said hoarsely, cowering away from him.

'Can't I? You should know above all people, my dear Amber, that a man is capable of having his sexual appetite aroused just by seeing a naked woman.'

Amber watched him warily, her eyes wide. Her mind

refused to think, seemed frozen inside her head. Then the words—sex, naked—penetrated her mind, and she struggled to get out of his grip, her eyes going desperately to the door.

'Didn't you hear me turn the key in the lock?' Dyson's voice tormented her as his eyes followed the direction hers had taken. 'No one is going to disturb us, and if I know Helen and Simon, they're going to be out for hours.'

'Let me go—— Please, please let me go,' Amber begged. 'I'll leave straight away—d-do anything else you ask, but please, please don't—don't do ...'

'You had fair warning,' he told her, as though instilling on her that she had brought this on herself.

'But Simon and I didn't ...' she began, only to feel herself being pulled inexorably closer to him.

'Shut up, and console yourself you're not getting out of here until ...' he left it in the air. Then she knew the time for pleading was over. 'Come here,' he said, and made it sound almost clinical. 'Come here and let's begin your punishment.'

'No!' she screamed, and that was all she had time for, because with an expertise she couldn't credit, her feet were taken from her and she found herself lying across him, his head coming down to meet hers.

She fought him like a wildcat, but her strength was nothing compared to his. She felt his mouth come down over hers and tried to bite him, but all that achieved was for him to take advantage of her open mouth, and his mouth was on hers, plundering there in a kiss like no other she could remember. Then his lips had left hers as he searched in the hollows of her throat, then cruelly back again to her mouth, and the feel of his mouth moving over hers had her fighting desperately; she couldn't breathe, she thought she was going to faint. 'Keep it up, Amber,' she heard him mutter against her lips, 'and I shan't have any trouble getting aroused for the likes of you.'

Hysterically the thought came to her that if only she could lie passive she could defeat him, for despite what he had said about a man having his sexual appetite aroused by seeing a naked woman, some part of her seemed to recognise in the little she knew of him that this wouldn't be the case if she could lie still and let him think he could do what he would with her. But she was too frightened, too out of control to just lie there and risk it.

Dyson's mouth left hers and her struggles took on fresh strength as he undid the top button of her shirt. Was this how it had been that other night? she wondered. But she still had no recollection. Then, horrifyingly, she was no longer lying across his lap, but beneath him on the wide settee. She felt his thighs hard against her own and tried to claw at his face, but he seemed to have twice as many hands as she as he grasped both her wrists in one and held them above her head, her breasts showing tautly beneath the stretched material of her shirt.

'Let's see what delights you are hiding, Amber my dear,' he drawled, his voice in cool contrast to his warm look. Amber wriggled her body, ignoring the feeling of pain in her lower spine, but she couldn't get away from the tight anchorage of his lean, well muscled length. 'Keep that up, my dear,' Dyson breathed smoothly, a hand going to the second button on her shirt, 'the movement of your body is having a *distinct* impression on my sexual urges.'

Crimson, his meaning clear as he adjusted his position on her, Amber almost went under as the look in his eyes told her he knew she had grasped his meaning. 'Now, my lovely,' he said, 'you have proof that I'm not joking,' and with that, the second button of her shirt came undone. As yet he had not touched her body with his hands, but as the third button came undone, she felt the whisper of his knuckles against her breast, and she pleaded with him anew.

'Please, Dyson, *please*,' she begged, 'don't do this— y-you're killing me!' His eyes fastened on hers as though he thought she was being over-dramatic, but Amber knew something inside her would die if he carried out his intent.

For a brief moment she thought her pleas had got through to him, for his hand stayed. 'Please,' she begged again, and then thinking if she told him the truth about last night he would see there was nothing to warrant this punishment. 'Simon ...'

She got no further. It was as though the mention of Simon's name was the red rag Dyson needed to spur him on. She saw the flame of fury in his eyes rekindle. 'You exaggerate my dear,' he said, and his lip curled in a sneer. 'I'm well aware you have suffered a "fate worse than death" before.' Then his hand was tearing at her shirt, her bra undone, and she was in an agony of embarrassment and shame as, still not touching her with his hands, Dyson moved his position to sit astride her, his weight heavy on her thighs as he gazed at her with a look on his face that could only be desire.

Then as he looked at her, she saw with disbelief the insolence which had been with him ever since he had touched her drop away. And her raw breathing quieted as she witnessed in his eyes a look of near artistic appreciation as he gazed at her nakedness.

'Your breasts are beautiful—the most beautiful I've ever seen,' seemed to be dragged from him, and some of his heat seemed to leave him as he bent his head and, almost as if paying homage, he kissed each rose-tipped pinnacle.

Only then did Amber's fight against him cease. She

had no idea whether her breasts were any more beautiful than the next woman's, but there was a shocked
stillness in the air, and though cringing with embarrassment, exposed as she was to his view, she whispered,
'Let me go, Dyson?' She was past pleading, but her
words came out huskily, a defeated note in her voice
because she knew she was asking in vain. Dyson was
beyond reasoning with, that she knew.

'I want to touch you—to hold you,' he said like someone entranced. 'I don't want to bruise your lovely
body.' He seemed to force his gaze from her breasts to
her face, and she saw something there that told her he
had a much greater sensitivity than ever she would
have believed.

'Yet you are bruising me, aren't you,' she whispered,
'and I think you're bruising yourself too, Dyson.' She
didn't know how she knew that, but at that moment
she was sure it was true.

His hand came slowly down as though he was
afraid the beauty of her would disappear before him
if he dared to touch the creamy swell of her, and
Amber held her breath as the hand hovered over her,
before control seemed to come to him from afar. Then
while she waited for that tormenting hand to come and
touch her smoothness, that same hand ceased its hover-
ing. But instead of closing over her breast, it moved
towards her throat and any sensitivity she had witnessed in him before was shattered completely, as he
muttered gratingly:

'You bewitching bitch.' His hand tightened against
her throat, and tears filled her eyes before he let go
his stranglehold. 'Do yourself up and get out of my
sight.'

Amber could barely believe it as he got up from her
and went to the window with his back towards her.
For a stunned second she just lay there uncompre-

hendingly, then she was galvanised into action lest he changed his mind. In a flash she was off the settee, her bra secured, her shaking fingers somehow matching the buttons on her shirt to the right buttonholes. She was at the door, turning the key to unlock it, when his voice came to her again.

'Try Simon on for size just once more and I shan't stop the next time,' he threatened, and turned round, his eyes going to her shirt, seeing the breasts he had called beautiful were once more hidden from him. 'You know what to expect if you don't behave yourself.'

Amber didn't wait to hear any more. She raced through the door, along the hall, and had her foot on the bottom stair before her agitated feelings guided her away and to the front door. She must keep away from her bedroom until Helen and Simon were back, she thought in confusion. Dyson had let her off, but there was no saying he wouldn't have second thoughts and come to seek her out.

Thoroughly shaken, she found herself outside, felt the cold of the December day hit her, but knew nothing would get her back inside the house, at least, not until she saw Helen and Simon. For the present she needed to get far away from Dyson as quickly as she could. Of their own volition her feet seemed to take her to the stables.

If Bill Ford, one of the stable hands, thought the pale-faced, bright-eyed girl was mad to come out on such a cold day in nothing but jeans and a shirt, then he kept his thoughts to himself, though it wouldn't surprise him if she didn't have to pay for such foolhardiness. Surely she couldn't be thinking of going riding dressed like that, she would freeze out on the moors, but apparently that was exactly what she did have in mind as she asked him if there was a horse she could borrow.

'There's Bluebell and High Noon,' he said after a second's hesitation. 'Red Diamond is being rested after going lame last week.'

Amber's eyes flicked to a magnificent stallion, Red Diamond, she thought, but Bill Ford, following her glance, corrected her on that point.

'That's Thunderbolt,' he told her, 'the master's horse,' and although he didn't say so, Amber knew she would only be allowed to ride Thunderbolt with Dyson's permission. Well, that was all right by her, she knew her capabilities better than to know she would be able to manage the snorting stallion. 'Done much riding, have you?' Bill enquired.

'Not lately,' Amber was forced to confess, becoming agitated that he was making no move to saddle up a horse for her—her need to put as much distance between her and Dyson urgent. 'Which horse may I have?'

'You'd better take Bluebell if you haven't ridden for some time—she's a gentle old lady.'

To Amber's mind, Bill took an age to saddle up the comfortable-looking Bluebell, but at last she was ready, and she was glad of his assistance in helping her to mount.

Slowly, getting the feel of Bluebell beneath her, Amber made her way out of the stableyard. She was feeling calmer now she was on the point of putting some distance between her and her odious host. She was aware she was shivering as she left the stableyard behind and took Bluebell at a walking pace out on to the fields that lay to the rear of the house, but the cold of the day biting into her was counteracted by the heat of her feelings as she relived the scene she had escaped from.

Her face flamed that Dyson had been prepared to strip her naked, to rape her as he had realised how terrified she was of him coming near her. She wouldn't forgive him ever. Even considering his actions had been purely because of what he thought she and Simon had been up to last night she couldn't forgive him. Even if she had been the tramp he had every right to think she was from his first encounter with her, he had no right to do what he had done.

She began to feel warmer as she tried Bluebell's trotting capabilities, then Bluebell broke into a canter, and suddenly all thoughts of Dyson and what she would like to do to him left her, as a devastating pain shot through her. It made her gasp and she couldn't think straight for a moment, then she pulled on the reins and immediately Bluebell obeyed, coming to a halt to await Amber's next instruction. The pain Amber had felt had been very real, but as she sat immobile on Bluebell's back, she breathed a sigh that she no longer felt anything. It was as she went to move to give the horse a pat for so promptly doing what she had been told that she realised she was in trouble. While sitting still, she felt nothing, but whenever she moved the pain hit her again. Gritting her teeth, she turned very slowly to see how far she had come. Moor View was still in her sights but seemed miles away, though common sense told her it couldn't be much more than half a mile. She would have to go back.

Agony accompanied every movement as she turned Bluebell round and headed her nose in the direction of home.

How long it took for her to walk Bluebell into the stableyard, Amber never knew. What she did know was that every movement of the horse's body beneath her was a knife going through her. She lost count of the times she reined the mare in, feeling the relief in the stillness from movement. Pain left her again as she

sat, her eyes searching for Bill. She would have to en-
list his help, for the only way she was going to get down
from Bluebell was with some assistance, that or allow
herself to fall off. Oh, where was he?

Her spirits lifted when she heard footsteps ringing
out on the cobbled yard. As yet she couldn't see him,
but soon he would be in her line of vision. Bravely
she summoned up a smile; she didn't want anyone to
know how forlorn she was feeling. Then as the footsteps came nearer and at last the figure of a man turned
the corner and came into the stableyard, the pretence
of a smile she was wearing rapidly disintegrated. For the
man saw her as soon as she saw him, and it wasn't Bill
Ford at all, but Dyson Silver, and the nearer he came,
the clearer the unmitigated fury on his face made itself
seen.

He was in riding clothes, and as his riding crop made
a vicious, give-me-strength swipe against his riding
boot, Amber had the very real feeling he was wishing
it had been her back the crop had come down upon.

'You idiot!' he yelled at her, coming to stand two
feet away from her and seeing she was almost blue with
cold. 'You stupid bloody idiot—haven't you any more
sense than to go out riding in this weather dressed like
that?'

CHAPTER SEVEN

'APPARENTLY not,' Amber retorted. She might be down, but she wasn't out—not yet she wasn't. And if he would only disappear, she felt sure it wouldn't be long before Bill came along. 'Anyway, I'd rather freeze to death than be within a quarter of a mile anywhere near to where you are.'

Dyson ignored her and took hold of Bluebell's reins. 'Get down from there,' he ordered. 'Get in the house and into a hot bath.'

The idea of a hot bath sounded nothing short of bliss. 'I'm waiting for Bill.'

'Someone else in trousers you can't leave alone?' Dyson had controlled his temper, but his sarcasm wasn't any less cutting. Amber ignored him and presented him with a stony face. 'Are you getting down or are you waiting for me to pull you down?' There was a smooth sarcasm in his voice now. 'As I recall, you can't bear me to touch you.' Then harshly, 'Get down!' he commanded.

'I will when you've gone.'

Not wasting time on further argument, Dyson reached up to her. 'Don't touch me!' she screamed before his hands could reach her waist, the movement of backing away from him causing that agonising pain to stab through her, and her pale face went ashen. But she kept her eyes on Dyson, and he too had lost some of his colour.

He breathed as though her terror of him shocked him. 'Does my touch affect you so badly?'

'It ... it's not that,' Amber found herself confessing,

when she had no intention of easing his mind if he had suddenly discovered he had a conscience over his treatment of her.

'Like hell it isn't,' he gritted, his colour returning. 'You become near-hysterical every time I come anywhere near you.'

Amber didn't think that was altogether true. It only happened when she thought she was in danger from his physical advances. Oh, where was Bill? It came to her then that whether Bill was here or not, she didn't stand very much chance of getting into the house without Dyson knowing something of her plight, for it would take some minutes for him to saddle up Thunderbolt and he was going to think it most suspiciously odd if she was still sitting on Bluebell's back when he was ready to go.

'Get into the house and take that bath,' Dyson said shortly, and there was an authority in his voice this time that said, like it or not, if she didn't do as he said, he would wrench her down and take her into the house by the scruff of her neck if she didn't obey him.

'I . . . I've—hurt my back.' There, it was out.

'You fell off Bluebell?' His very tone said that was an impossibility.

'No, it's—it's an old injury,' and then because she had all his attention on her now, and in a way it was a relief to have told him, 'I—I thought it wouldn't hurt to . . .'

'That's why you didn't go riding with Helen and Simon, isn't it?' Then shrewdly, 'But you wanted to get as far away from me as possible.'

Amber didn't answer—she couldn't deny it, but suddenly it seemed very stupid to have taken the risk when common sense had told her not to try riding just yet. Only . . .

Dyson had obviously decided that now was not the

time for further discussion. 'We'd better get you down from there,' he said, and his hands came up once more and this time settled on her waist.

'Don't move me,' Amber told him hurriedly, then because it sounded very much as if she was giving him orders, and she wasn't sure how he would take that: 'If ... if you could just hold me steady ...'

'All right,' he said, and she was surprised at the mildness in his tone. 'I won't jar you—you come to me in your own time.'

Every movement torture, though she tried to keep it from showing in her face, Amber leaned over to him. She knew without trying it would be impossible to lift her one leg over the saddle. Then slowly, with Dyson taking more and more of her weight, she had her arms around his neck and was glad when the side of her face came against his, that he couldn't see the agony in her eyes she could no longer disguise.

'I'll step back and take you with me,' Dyson said. 'Ready?'

'Ready,' said Amber, and clutched hard at him as she and Bluebell parted company and she was resting up against him, her arms still around his neck.

'You're in agony, aren't you?' Dyson said when she made no move to break away from him.

She wanted to say, It only hurts when I laugh, anything to lighten the situation, but it was beyond her. 'I don't seem to be able to stand up on my own,' she whispered.

Then there was no need for her to try and stand at all, for very gently Dyson picked her up in his arms and was losing no more time as he carried her into the house. He didn't speak again until he had carried her into her bedroom, and there he deposited her on the small bedroom chair, before going into the bathroom. Amber could hear the bath water running, but for the moment it was enough just to sit there and not feel any pain.

'I'll get Mrs Randle to come and see to you while I get the doctor,' he said, his face stern.

'No!' Amber said sharply, and had Dyson looking at her. She saw from his expression that he would brook no argument. 'Please don't trouble anyone—please, Dyson!' He looked set to ignore her, but since he had paused on his way to the door, Amber went on hurriedly, 'Mrs Randle has enough to do, and besides —I—I feel terrible because it was my own stupidity that brought this on.'

Dyson squatted down by the side of her so that he could see into her face. 'I think I'm partly to blame as well, aren't I?'

Pink colour washed over her face, and she couldn't look at him. 'Please,' she said again. 'I'll be all right once I've had a rest—I've had something similar before.'

Dyson looked ready to ask for more details, then seemed to know that now wasn't the time to go into that. 'All right,' he conceded when she had been sure he wouldn't. 'I'll let you have your own way over Mrs Randle—but I must insist on having a doctor to see you.'

'My doctor is in Exeter and I don't want him coming all this way to see me when I know I shall be all right again by the time he gets here,' Amber said stubbornly. But she found that Dyson could be equally stubborn.

'There's no need to call your doctor out. I'll get my man to come and take a look at you,' he said as if the whole argument stopped there. 'You said the pain you're in now is the result of an old injury—give me the name of your doctor and I'll get Dr Farley to phone him so he can be acquainted with the details of your case before he gets here.'

Against her will Amber found herself saying, 'It's Dr Cresswell,' and when Dyson had this piece of information from her, he went into the bathroom, turned off the taps and returned to her, helping her to stand. Feeling she would look like the Hunchback of Notre Dame if she attempted to walk, Amber was glad when Dyson picked her up and carried her into the bathroom, where he placed her on the bathroom stool.

'I'll probably be as right as ninepence once I've had a hot bath,' she said, feeling tense suddenly that he hadn't moved to leave her on her own.

'Let's hope so,' he said easily, and without more ado his hands came down to help her undress.

'No!' It came out much more sharply than she had intended, but had the same effect that she wanted. 'I can manage on my own.'

'It looks like it,' Dyson said sourly.

'I can.'

'You can't bear to have me touch you, can you?' he grated.

'No, I can't,' she snapped back. But not for the reasons he thought. She was aware that there was nothing remotely sexual in his touch this time; his sole aim was to help her where she could not help herself. But no one apart from the medical staff at the hospital, and Uncle James as her doctor, had seen those terrible scars on her lower back, and since Dyson hadn't been aware of her back injury until she had told him, he must have made love to her that time without seeing them either. He thought her breasts were beautiful, and it shook her that she didn't want him to know that the rest of her body was not.

'I can manage by myself,' she repeated stonily, and couldn't look at him.

'It's a great pity I'm not Simon, isn't it,' he snarled above her head. 'I'm sure you'd have no qualms about letting him help you.'

Amber didn't move until she heard the outer door slam. He could be a pig when he chose, she thought wearily, as with tortoiselike movements she undressed and, using her arms for support, lowered herself into the steaming bath. Though she had to admit she would never have made it to her room if he hadn't carried her, for walking until she had the kinks out of her back was beyond her.

It was sheer bliss to feel the heat of the water on her body, and she was sorely tempted, when the heat began to go from it, to run some more water from the hot tap, before deciding she had better get out and into bed. She wasn't sure she trusted Dyson not to send Mrs Randle up to her, for all he had said he would let her have her way on that issue.

But thinking of getting out of the bath and actually accomplishing that feat, Amber found, were two totally different matters. Getting into the bath hadn't been easy. To get out of it, she found, was quite impossible. Still, she wasn't ready to admit defeat. She drained the water out of the bath, and as whenever she made the smallest progress she only slipped painfully back on the shiny porcelain, she managed to grab hold of a hand towel hanging on a nearby rail and pulled at it, then proceeded to spread it beneath her hoping it would give her more leverage.

After ten minutes, Amber at last admitted defeat. She could have wept, almost did, but allowed herself only one heartfelt moan of despair, hoping that after all Dyson had thought to send Mrs Randle to her. By now he would think she was safely tucked up in bed, instead of which she was sitting here, damp, miserable, and despite the central heating, getting colder by the minute.

Her heart lifted when she heard her bedroom door open, and she no longer felt like crying. Mrs Randle would help her. But it wasn't Mrs Randle's voice that reached her from the other side of the bathroom door. The tones she heard were very masculine, and for all she thought Dyson had washed his hands of her when she had told him she could manage on her own, it was Dyson who had come into her room expecting her to be in bed.

'Amber—are you all right in there?'

Quickly Amber dragged the hand towel from beneath her, holding it in front of her because she knew he wouldn't care tuppence about any feelings of modesty she might have.

'I'm ... I'm stuck,' she said, and knew she had been right—he didn't care a button about her feelings of modesty. For the door was pushed inwards, and he stared down at her resigned, wide-eyed face, saw she was holding an inadequate soaking wet towel against the front of her, her shoulders bare. Without a word he turned from her and she thought he was going to leave her, until she saw he was taking an over-large bath towel from off the heated rail.

'How long have you been sitting there like that?' he asked, turning back to her.

'It seems like a year,' Amber told him, striving for humour but knowing she was near to giving way to tears.

The bath towel came around her shoulders, its delicious warmth sheer heaven, then Dyson was saying, 'Put an arm up,' and she thought she must be going delirious or something, for she obeyed without question, still holding the soggy hand towel in front of her.

She felt the warmth of the towel coming under her arm, saw that Dyson was pulling it in front of her, caught on to what he had in mind, and with the front of her now decently covered with the end of the bath towel, she let go her hold on the clammy hand towel and lifted her other arm for him to fold the other end of the bath towel in front of her. She felt his fingers warm against her skin as he tucked the end in and wondered what happened now.

'Put your arms up,' he instructed, 'and clasp your hands at the back of my neck.' Dumbly she complied with his every order. 'Now grit your teeth,' he said, and as Amber looked at him startled at this latest instruction, she saw the tight-lipped look disappear to be replaced by an encouraging smile. Then she knew the reason why she should grit her teeth, for he was lifting her out of the bath, and for all his movements were unhurried, she needed to grit her teeth to stop her from crying out in pain.

On their way out of the bathroom, Dyson paused to collect another towel hanging on the rail, and once in the bedroom he asked, 'Is it going to hurt you to lie on your front?'

'N—no,' she stammered.

She felt his fingers loosening the tucked-in fold of the towel around her, but before she could have time to think, he was placing her gently down on the bed, with the towel still covering her. He gave her no time to wonder further, but immediately set to work giving her feet and that part of her legs visible beneath her covering - a thorough if careful towelling. Warmth began to seep through her feet and legs when his ministrations were done. Then the glow that had been beginning to start that this nightmare would soon be over disappeared as Dyson attempted to take her covering from her.

'No,' she said quickly. 'I'll—I'll be all right now, thank you.'

There was a tense silence behind her, before he said, 'I'm well aware that you shudder at the thought of me touching you,' his voice was impersonal, 'but you're chilled to the marrow—I assure you my only interest in you is to try and ward off anything else unpleasant that might befall you if we don't get your blood circulating again. Now be a good girl and try and make my job easier. I promise I won't hurt your back.'

Reluctantly Amber gave in. She couldn't argue against the common sense of what he said. He had no interest in her, he had made that abundantly clear. All that bothered him was that he ensured he didn't have her cluttering up his house after the holiday was over should she go down with pleurisy or the like. Still the same there was no way she could relax knowing that soon he would see those ugly scars.

Having got the ends of the towel from under her, Dyson did not take her covering from her completely, but pulled it back over her lower half while he set to work methodically bringing first one arm back to life and then the other, making her shoulders and upper back tingle, and only when that was done did he begin to uncover the rest of her. Her movements to grab hold of the bath towel to cover herself again before it was dropped to the floor was quick, painful and instinctive, but she was too late. She knew from the way his hands didn't at once begin their work that the three six- or seven-inch scars going in opposite directions from her lower spine and across her buttocks had shocked him. She wanted to say something, anything, but couldn't utter a sound.

Dyson couldn't quite stifle the exclamation that was wrenched from his lips, and Amber could have wept that he thought her ugly. Then that half of her was receiving the same treatment her legs, arms and shoulders had received, only when the towel touched her scars, his touch was infinitely gentle. Then his arm was coming across her bare shoulders, and she tingled afresh as his fingers gripped her.

'I'll help you to turn over,' he said matter-of-factly, no evidence at all in his voice that her scars had shaken him.

'I—can't let you,' Amber protested.

The situation was more than intimate as it was, and even though Dyson had gazed his fill at her breasts only hours ago, she knew she would rather die of raging pneumonia than allow him to see her again. She thought he was going to snap and snarl at her, was ready for it, and almost went into shock herself when he said quietly:

'All right—— Nightie under your pillow?'

Relief flooded through her that he was still being kind to her. 'Yes,' she answered huskily, and in next to no time Dyson was pulling her nightie over her head, and while he went to the other side of the bed to open the sheets, although every movement made her bite her lip, she pulled her nightdress down the front of her. Then he was picking her up once more, and mercifully she was beneath the covers, and he was returning the towels to the bathroom.

He came back with a glass of water in his hand, and delving into his pocket withdrew a bottle of tablets. 'A couple of these should lessen the pain,' he told her, unscrewing the cap, and she realised he must have gone to fetch them when he had left her in the bathroom.

'I've pain-killers of my own,' Amber said, hating suddenly all the trouble she was putting him to.

Dyson pocketed the bottle. 'In your bag?' he asked, looking about him for her handbag.

'In my case—it's on the shelf in the wardrobe.'

'You take pain-killers regularly?' he asked as he slid back the wardrobe door and extracted her case.

'Oh no—I haven't taken any for ages,' she said, feeling foolish. 'I only popped them in because I thought if I didn't I might need them, but if I brought them with me, I wouldn't.' She knew that garbled explanation would sound ridiculous to a sophisticated man like him, but Dyson didn't look as though he thought it ridiculous.

'A sort of good luck charm?' he said, and bent down to her case.

He found the tablets without difficulty. The small bottle was all that was in there, Amber thought, until she remembered, and embarrassed colour flooded her face as Dyson stood up and showed her he had found not only the tablets, but the Christmas present bearing his name.

'Didn't you think I deserved to have this?' he asked, but he was smiling as he dropped the package on the bed and set about giving her the prescribed dosage he read off the label on the bottle of tablets.

Amber felt the strength of his arm supporting her as she swallowed the two magic potions that would get to work on her in no time. Then lying once more on her side, the most comfortable position, she found, she apologised for not giving him his present before, and he accepted it so charmingly, seeming to understand her shyness at the time. And suddenly he was no longer the ogre she had thought him, and as he pulled the bedroom chair up to the bed and looked set to sit with her for a while, Amber found she was glad to have him there. The gift he must have seen for Simon was not mentioned, and she thought better than to bring his name up.

'How are you feeling now?' Dyson asked quietly.

'Fine,' Amber answered automatically, and as an eyebrow raised disbelievingly at her, she gave a shamefaced grin. 'Well, there have been days when I've felt better, but it only hurts when I move.'

'Good,' he said, and there was a wealth of charm coming through, and if she hadn't felt so guilty about having to take to her bed in someone else's house, she thought with wonder, she would have felt completely relaxed.

Perhaps the tablets she had swallowed were making her unwind, she thought, though she couldn't think they were that fast acting. But when Dyson's question came, it didn't have her clamming up as she would have thought she would have done.

'How did you come to injure your back, Amber?'

She supposed she had been expecting that question ever since he had first seen her scars, but now it was here it wasn't nearly as painful to tell him—not until it came to telling him that her parents had not been so lucky and that they had died in that rock fall. Quietly she told him about the accident, her eyes clouding over at the memory of the last time she had seen her mother and father. 'We were very close,' she ended huskily.

'How long ago was this? Your scars look quite recent.'

That was something she didn't want to tell him. He would know from her reply that her meeting with him had happened soon after. But as he pinned her with his dark-eyed look, she knew there was no escape; he had already discerned that her scars were not all that old.

'It happened in July,' she mumbled, and saw a calculating look appear in his eye.

'Two months before we met,' he said, having no trouble with his arithmetic. 'You couldn't have been out of hospital for very long.'

'A week,' she confessed, and felt the stirrings of disquiet growing within her. She didn't want to carry on with this conversation.

But apparently Dyson was going to leave nothing buried. 'So you were still convalescing when you sat perched on that bar stool?'

'Yes,' she replied, though his question didn't need an answer, she felt compelled to defend herself. 'I ... I was feeling pretty low that day—I ...' Oh, what could she say in her defence? Her conduct had been every bit that of the trollop he had called her, there was no defence against that.

'So you were fed up at having been out of circulation for two months and decided to make up for lost time?'

If he wanted to believe that he could get on with it, Amber thought, all feelings of being at ease with him vanishing under his questioning. Stubbornly she kept her lips firmly closed. But Dyson wasn't ready to let her wriggle off his hook, she thought mutinously as he continued, his voice returning to the cool cynical tones she was accustomed to from him.

'You must have been in pain still,' he commented, and she guessed he must have gathered that from what she had told him of her injuries.

'I was taking pain-killers regularly at the time. I took more when—when we—when we reached your room.'

She saw his eyes narrow at that, but he went on relentlessly, 'Ah yes, my room,' then harshly, 'It's a pity your aversion to me didn't make itself felt before we got that far.'

'I haven't—I ...' Oh, now he was making her feel

guilty about that too, and instead of firing back at him she found herself thinking she was being unfair to him. After all, it couldn't be very nice for him having her shrivelling up into a ball of fear every time it looked as though he was going to touch her. That she should be thinking this way when only hours earlier she had thought she hated him and would like to see him suffer didn't seem at all strange to her just then. 'I haven't got an aversion to you,' she told him, and at his look that clearly said, 'Liar', 'I haven't, honestly.' It seemed important he should believe her, though for the life of her she couldn't think why. 'Well, not in the way you think I have.'

'No?' He still didn't believe her, that much was obvious.

'No,' she repeated, and took a deep breath, her fingers plucking at the bed covers, and unable to look at him, she explained haltingly, 'Th-that night—you know, that night in y-your room—well,' she flicked a glance at him and saw she had his full attention, 'well, I can remember going to your room with you—remember the bathroom—but for the life of me I-I can't remember what we talked about.' Her voice dropped to a whisper, the hand plucking at the covers growing feverish, as her voice tailed off, '... or even if we talked.'

'You're telling me it's all a blank?'

She couldn't look at him, his voice didn't sound as if he was surprised, but then she suspected he was keeping his voice even so as not to make her feel worse than she felt and so clam up on him completely.

'I c-can't remember a thing apart from being in that room with you, going to the bathroom and taking some more tablets because I ...' Her voice petered out, she wasn't prepared to go any further.

'Because ...?' Dyson prompted her. Amber was sure

she wasn't going to tell him, and then felt his hand come to settle over hers as she fidgeted with the bed covers. His touch was cool, and so gentle, immediately her fingers ceased their mutilations, and she looked into eyes that bore no trace of the hardness she expected to see there. 'Go on,' he urged quietly. 'You took some more tablets because . . .'

Amber looked down at the hand that lay over hers. A sensitive hand, gentle, with long artistic fingers. 'Well, you know anyway,' she said huskily.

'What do I know, Amber?'

'A man always knows,' she said, then thinking perhaps her information might be at fault, though sure it wasn't. 'Doesn't he?' She couldn't look at him at all now as searing hot colour burned every part of her.

'A man always knows what?' he pressed.

It all came out in a rush then. 'A man always knows when he takes a v-virgin to bed,' she said, and galloped on, barely noticing that the hand over hers had clenched and was bruising her knuckles. 'I knew you'd find out it was m-my first time—and I didn't want to kick up a fuss if it—if you—if you hurt me, s-so I took some pain-killers so you wouldn't be mad with me.' Suddenly she became aware that her hand was being crushed beneath his. 'You're hurting me,' she muttered, and saw her hand was white from the pressure of his when he took his hand away.

'Oh Amber,' Dyson said, and his voice sounded hoarse, so that she couldn't bear to look at him to find out what he meant by that.

All she knew was that she had to get it all said now, and quickly. 'Like I said, I couldn't remember and—and when I woke up the next morning—you were there, and—well, I was feeling a bit sick with myself, so I took a taxi home. I've heard of people having amnesia when something happens they would rather forget.

Don't tell me,' she said quickly. 'I don't want to know anything that happened in that b-bed.'

'Are you sure you wouldn't rather know?' Dyson asked, and his voice sounded peculiar in her ears, and she was convinced suddenly that the time she had spent with him had been awful. Had she kicked and screamed, been frightened, terrified, had second thoughts?

'I'm sure,' she told him. 'I beg of you not to tell me.' A shudder went through her as all sorts of possibilities went through her mind. 'What I've been leading up to tell you is that not knowing anything of that night— when you went to kiss me that first time, it came to me that your touch might trigger off my memory.'

'And it didn't?' Whatever had affected Dyson was gone from him now, for his voice was back to normal, and his face when she dared a peep at him gave nothing away as to whether his memories of that night were distasteful or not.

'No.'

'And that's the only reason you can't bear me to touch you?' he asked gently.

'Mainly that,' she said. 'I didn't want you to see the ugly scars on my back either.'

Dyson didn't tell her they weren't ugly, and she valued his honesty, but he did repeat what she had been told in hospital. 'They'll soon fade and be barely noticeable.' She wished she could believe him, for all no one else was likely to see them. He then went on to make her blush again by referring to what had taken place between them that morning. 'I think we've proved from that exhibition that your memory of that night isn't going to come back,' he said, and she couldn't be sure, but she thought there was a note of self-loathing in his voice when he referred to that morning. Mutely she nodded her head in agreement of what he had just said, then he was saying kindly, 'Don't worry at it any more, Amber—Helen went a bit wild when her mother died, so I do have some idea of the phase you went through.'

It seemed that Dyson had swung completely from the man who had believed she was a tramp to now believing she was a young woman who needed gentle understanding. But it wasn't gentle understanding Amber needed. She had been totally wrong in what she had done, and if Dyson could understand her actions and virtually say 'there, there' and call it a phase she had gone through, she couldn't be so forgiving of herself. Always, she thought, she would feel second-hand, and she wasn't having him patronising her either.

'Oh, you've not been the only one,' she lied, indignation in the set look of her face that he could treat having taken her virginity as if it was just one of those things. She had dreamed of going to some mystically romantic husband untouched, and had flayed herself raw these past few months that if and when that romantic figure appeared, she would have to confess that he wasn't the first.

'No?' Dyson queried, his voice growing tight. Then smoothly as if he wasn't ready to believe her, 'There've been other men since me?'

'Of course.' She didn't hesitate.

'Tell me, Amber, did you feel any pain with any of your lovers?'

'In my back, do you mean?' she asked uncertainly.

'No, Amber, I don't mean in your back,' he said succinctly.

'Oh,' she said, colouring hotly. Well, he needn't think he was going to catch her out so easily. 'Of course not,' she said, convincingly, she thought, and couldn't understand that it looked, when she flicked the minutest peep at him, as though he was going to grin at her answer. That grin was only a fleeting impression, for his face was stern the next time she looked at him.

'Well, now we've aired a few bogeys, I think it's time you settled down to rest. It shouldn't be too long before lunch is ready.' He stood up to go, and Amber eyed him warily. 'Since you no longer have any fear of my kisses, and since you look so delectable lying there ...' he didn't finish, but bent over her and laid a whisper of a kiss against her mouth, before taking up the gift she had omitted to give him on Christmas Day, and left her. Her mind was too jumbled by all that had been said for rest to come easily.

Nevertheless, she had been asleep when Maureen brought her lunch tray in. 'I'm sorry to cause you all this trouble,' she apologised to the willing Maureen.

'No trouble at all, miss,' Maureen replied. 'We're all sorry you've hurt your back.' She then went on to give Amber such a graphic description of how badly her father had been when he had had lumbago that Amber actually winced for him as she was telling her.

She had barely finished her meal before Helen came in, and after commiserating with her told her they had had their lunch ages ago. 'I wanted to come up and see you straight away, but Dyson said not to as you were asleep.' Amber felt the stirrings of unease; he could only know that if he had peeped in on her. 'He asked Mrs Randle to keep your lunch hot for you,' Helen confided.

'I'm sorry to be all this bother ...' Amber began.

'Rot! Nobody's ever ill in this house—we're all dying to try our hand at the Florence Nightingale bit.' Helen plumped up Amber's pillows as though to prove it, then helped her, hanging grimly on to her, to the bathroom, assisting her to make the same painful return journey back to bed.

'I'll be up tomorrow,' Amber said gamely, but saw

from Helen's look that she didn't believe her.

'You'll be better off in bed, actually,' she told her. 'Dyson's got Simon in his study at the moment, and if things follow their normal course, neither of them will be fit company for a couple of days—black clouds are forecast!'

Dyson had once referred to her bedroom as being not unlike a fairground, Amber recalled, and no sooner had Helen gone than Dyson himself appeared. But there was nothing of the dark cloud about him when he asked how she was feeling after her sleep.

About to say 'Fine', she saw an eyebrow begin to ascend, and gave him a shamefaced smile as she amended it to, 'Better, thank you.'

She watched him as he walked over to the window; from the angle she was lying he looked taller than ever, and broad with it. 'Right,' he said, 'we'll see what the doctor makes of you.'

'Doctor?' She had thought he had forgotten all about having said he would get his doctor to take a look at her.

'Doctor,' he confirmed with a look that said she didn't know him very well if she thought he had forgotten. 'A car has just pulled on to the drive. If I'm not mistaken it will be him. I'll go and show him up.'

Left to herself, Amber wondered what Dr Farley would be like. Convinced she would be better tomorrow, she felt a humbug at his having been called away from his family, on Boxing Day too.

But when the door opened and Dyson came into the room, Amber looked past him and saw a man who was dearly familiar to her. Afterwards she thought it must have been the shock of seeing him when she had thought him to be thirty miles away in Exeter that brought the tears to her eyes.

'Dr Cresswell insisted on coming to see for himself

what you'd been up to,' Dyson explained, and though she would rather anyone see her cry but Dyson, Amber exclaimed:

'Uncle James—— Oh, Uncle James!' and promptly burst into tears.

CHAPTER EIGHT

'AMBER!' James Cresswell tried not to let his concern
for her show, but she was dear to him and her distress
tugged at his heartstrings. 'What is it, my dear?' he
asked, hurrying over to her bed. Amber wasn't the sort
to give way easily. He had seen her grin and bear much
more than she must be suffering at the moment, for he
had been informed as he had climbed the stairs with
the tall severe-looking man who was now watching
closely from his position at the foot of the bed that
Amber's setback had come about after she had been
out riding, of all things.

'Oh, Uncle James,' Amber said again, and wished she
could stop crying, for although Uncle James had seen
her in tears before, Dyson Silver never had.

James Cresswell suddenly remembered the last time
he had seen Amber in tears, and thought he had
guessed the reason for her uncontrollable weeping.
'Listen to me, Amber,' he said, and his stern voice had
her paying him attention. 'You aren't going to die,
child. I thought you'd been convinced of that—thought
that notion had been cleared out of your mind. Now
come along, mop your eyes. If you're still not convinced I'll take you personally to see Dr. Phillips, and
we'll have an open discussion with your case papers
and everyone who attended you at the hospital if need
be. Your condition *isn't* terminal, Amber,' he stressed.

Amber stared at him, her tears stopped rolling down
her cheeks and clung wetly to her long lashes. And as
what he said penetrated, she began to feel dreadful,
for she could see if she was upset, though what she'd

got to cry about she couldn't think, then she was being most unfair, for Uncle James looked very upset too. She looked to the foot of the bed and saw with a shock that immediately dried her tears that Dyson had a grey look to him and that his hands were clenched on to one of the corner posts of her bed almost as though he needed to have something to hang on to.

'Believe me, Amber,' James Cresswell was saying.

'Oh yes—yes, I do,' Amber said quickly, wrenching her eyes away from Dyson. 'I'm sorry, Uncle James, I wasn't crying about that.' She saw him looking at her closely—if she had any lingering doubts he wanted to hear all about them. 'I know I was an idiot thinking Mr Phillips was talking about me—but I believed you when you told me before.' She hoped he wasn't going to ask if that wasn't the reason for her tears then what was, for she couldn't have said.

James Cresswell seemed satisfied at that. 'If you're positive,' he said. 'Well, young lady, I'd better take a look and see what you've been up to.'

Amber's eyes flew to Dyson's. His colour seemed normal now—she could have imagined he had looked slightly grey, but ... Dyson returned her look, his mouth unsmiling; he seemed to know she didn't want him there while Uncle James examined her.

'I'll leave you to it,' he said shortly, and strode sharply from the room.

James Cresswell's examination of Amber was thorough and though the need to cause her pain was unavoidable as his fingers probed over her, he was able to tell her that in his opinion it was only a minor reversion.

'I shouldn't advise you to try your hand at riding again for a while,' he said dryly, causing Amber to look shamefaced that she had done so in the first place. 'The spinal column, as indeed the whole region of the back is, is such a mass of muscle, fibre and tissue that it isn't easy to pinpoint the exact trouble,' he went on to explain, 'but I think we'll find you've simply tackled too much too soon and this is nature's way of saying "I'm not ready yet". Stay in bed tomorrow to give your muscles the chance to rest,' he added, much to Amber's dismay.

'But, Uncle James ...' She got no further as James Cresswell gave her a look that said, 'Who's the doctor here, you or me?' 'All right,' she agreed, wanting to ask him to take her home as the thought of the trouble she was putting everyone to struck her again. But she knew even if she did voice her wish to return to Exeter, Uncle James would insist on taking her to his home; he wouldn't let her go back to an empty house by herself.

He stayed chatting to her for some minutes before getting to his feet, and Amber gave him her heartfelt thanks for coming all this way to see her.

'You're one of my favourite patients,' he told her with a smile. 'Now take my advice, Amber, and stay in bed tomorrow.'

Amber found she wasn't left to her own devices for very long. Footsteps outside in the corridor had her eyes going to the door, and where her first thought was that it was Dyson coming back to see her, she couldn't understand the flutter inside her that died when the door was cautiously opened and Helen poked her head round.

'Ah, you're awake,' she said, coming into the room and closing the door. 'I saw Dr Cresswell go into the study with Dyson ten minutes ago and since there's no sign of anyone coming out, I thought I'd come and ask *you* what the doctor's verdict was if you were awake.'

'Oh, it's nothing serious,' Amber replied, wondering what Dyson and Uncle James had got to say to each other that could take ten minutes—perhaps they were having a drink together; Uncle James might let himself go seeing that it was Christmas. 'I don't hurt at all if I lie still, and Uncle James says I'll be fine by Saturday.'

'Oh, good,' said Helen, and followed on, 'So that's your Uncle James. We never did get down to swopping confidences, did we? I hadn't a clue that you'd been in an accident and had to take things carefully.' Amber felt guilty that she hadn't said anything until Helen said, 'Still, that's what's made us friends, I suppose— both of us respecting each other's need to be private.'

Amber was beginning to like Helen more as she got to know her, and Helen stayed with her for half an hour until the door opened and Simon came in. Amber experienced that fluttering sensation again as the door opened until she saw it was Simon.

'How's the patient?' he asked, coming in and sitting himself down on the bed, until Helen told him to get up.

'You're jarring Amber, plonking yourself down on the bed like some ungainly camel,' she reproved him.

'Sorry,' he said, and got up to collect the pink velvet-topped dressing-table stool, then joined in a three-cornered conversation until after some minutes he said to Helen, 'I wanted to have a word with Amber alone.'

'Secrets?' asked Helen, but seeing Simon was not to be drawn, she stood up. 'Curiouser and curiouser,' she said. 'I'll see you later, Amber, and you can tell me what Simon wants to speak to you alone about.'

'Scram,' ordered Simon, and not a bit put out, Helen went.

Amber looked at Simon and saw he couldn't meet her eyes. Then she saw the colour come up under his skin and felt sorry for him as she realised what it was he had to say to her that he didn't want Helen to hear.

'It's all right, Simon,' she said softly, trying to help

him out. 'You'd had a little too much to drink, I think ...'

'It's not all right.' Simon refused to have his load of guilt lightened. 'I behaved very badly coming into your room last night—you're my sister's guest too. I felt the biggest heel out when I woke up this morning and it all came back. I don't deserve your forgiveness.' He smiled sheepishly. 'But you will forgive me, won't you?'

Who wouldn't? That little-boy-lost look was on his face again. 'Of course.' Amber's reply was automatic until she saw Simon wouldn't feel better until he'd been choked off about it. 'Only never do it again,' she added, adopting a stern attitude.

Simon cheered up at once. 'Oh, I won't, believe me.' He then went on to tell her about Kit Lancaster's party, saying he wished she had gone with him, and confiding that of all the foul luck Dyson had seen him leaving her room last night. This was no news to Amber; Dyson had drawn his own conclusions from seeing Simon leaving her bedroom, and she had no wish to relive what had happened when she had gone into Dyson's study.

'I knew I was in for a rocket when Dyson said he wanted to see me this morning,' Simon confessed, 'and boy, did I get one! I hadn't any defence either. Come to think of it, I don't think I said more than two words. I know you're not the willing sort, but it would have made no difference had you been—I didn't get the chance to say nothing had happened between us— Dyson read me chapter and verse, and then went on to tell me about your back injury, underlining Helen's opinion that I'm a clumsy camel, and saying that I'm not to give way to any inclinations I have for horseplay while you're around. By then of course I'd forgotten I was going to tell him that you in your lady-like fashion had given me the big E—elbow,' he elucidated for

Amber's benefit. 'But I'll tell him as soon as the right moment comes up.'

'Don't,' Amber said quickly.

'Don't?' Simon questioned. 'I must, Amber,' he said, showing her he was learning a sense of responsibility. 'I can't let Dyson go around thinking you welcomed my coming into your room last night.'

Knowing she had already deliberately let Dyson think exactly that, something inside her made her want Dyson to go on believing it. She didn't even know why, and didn't have time to analyse it because Simon was waiting for her to give him one concrete reason why he shouldn't let Dyson know he hadn't been her lover.

'Er—I've had a word with him myself and explained,' she said. 'It wouldn't do any good to open the subject up again.'

Simon seemed to need little persuasion after that to give in. 'All right,' he conceded, and went on to tell her, 'Actually, to give the devil his due, Dyson doesn't often haul me over the coals these days.' He paused reflectively and didn't have to go back further than the summer to recall the last time. 'We had one hell of a ding-dong the last time I was home!'

Amber had known that, it was part of her reason for being here, though since Helen had refrained from telling her what the row had been about, save to say she thought Simon had been in the wrong, Amber didn't expect him to tell her, but she discovered Simon had none of the inhibitions his sister had.

'When I came home this time I didn't know whether to throw my hat in first.' Simon saw Amber was intrigued and went on to tell her that the row had all started after he had wrapped his sports car round a tree. 'Entirely my own fault,' he said carelessly. 'A little too much vino—anyway, I wanted to have another sports car.' He sidetracked for a while as he went on to tell her about 'this fantastic job' before returning to what he had been telling her. 'I knew the car I wanted cost the earth, but I was furious when Dyson said I couldn't have it. He reminded me that I already had two endorsements on my licence and said he wasn't forking out to buy some high-powered car I couldn't handle and in which he was sure I would end up killing myself. Then he made me livid by saying he'd pay for a sports car for me when I'd learned some sense—apart from my allowance I'm broke until I'm twenty-five, or I'd never have asked him,' he inserted. 'Anyway, Dyson had transferred some shares into my name when I was twenty-one on the understanding that I wouldn't touch them. But I was so mad about not being allowed to have the car I wanted, I went and sold most of them.'

'Oh dear,' said Amber, not sure what else she could have said. Both brothers seemed to be stubborn, but Simon appeared to be hotheaded as well.

'Oh dear is right,' he said ruefully. 'I was as sorry as hell afterwards, because I knew Dyson had been working all hours on a deal a competitor was trying to muscle in on. He'd already asked if he could have the backing of my shares to help the deal go through—all high finance and way above my head—but I'd said yes. Of course he found out what I'd done. Thinking about it later I think he was more upset that I'd broken his trust than by the fact that he'd discovered the opposition had snapped up the shares.'

'Oh dear,' Amber said again, feeling slightly sick as she visualised all hell breaking loose when Dyson had tackled Simon about it. 'So—er—the deal didn't go through?'

'Oh, but it did—— You don't know Dyson if you think he'd let a little thing like the impossible put him off.' Simon's face took on a look of admiration, which

told her that for all the stepbrothers had a tendency
to rub each other up the wrong way, there was an
underlying brotherly love between them. 'I don't know
how he did it, but Dyson pulled it off all right. Though
I think at that point some of the "sense" he'd been
talking about finally got through to my old grey matter
—I didn't have the heart to buy the sports car after
that.'

Helen coming in to see if there was anything Amber
needed put a stop to anything else Simon would have
told her. 'How can Amber need anything when I'm
here?' Simon joked, but he got to his feet when Helen
told him he couldn't watch while she straightened
Amber's bed. 'You're both spoilsports,' he said, as he
was shooed out of the room.

When Amber settled down to go to sleep that night,
she reflected that the whole household had put themselves out to see that she wasn't lonely. Helen had been
a constant visitor, and Simon had popped in to see her
after dinner. Mrs Randle had been too, and Maureen
had seemed in no hurry to go when she had returned to
collect her dinner things. It all helped to make her feel
part of a family again, and her only regret was that
Dyson hadn't been anywhere near since his departure
when Uncle James had looked ready to examine her.

The thought that she was sorry Dyson hadn't been to
see her was shattering enough for her to give him some
very serious thought. How well he had looked after
her since he had helped her from Bluebell's back. It
seemed to cancel out everything that had gone before
—though of all that had passed between them, she
would never be able to forget he had been her lover,
nor would she ever forget that scene in his study this
morning.

Movement was less painful now, and slowly she adjusted her position. On one hand she wished she felt

more sleepy, on the other she was afraid to go to sleep for fear the nightmare she had had last night would return. She didn't want to stay awake, for her thoughts of Dyson—and for some reason he seemed to dominate her waking thoughts—were taking a confusing turn. Yet to sleep and dream that nightmare again wasn't welcome either.

Amber was torn between the thought that she had better turn her light out, and the thought that she didn't want to, when the door opened and she saw Dyson standing there. The fluttering sensation she had experienced throughout the afternoon and evening when she had thought everyone coming in to see her was Dyson set up again inside her, making her feel agitated when he came over to her bed.

'Not asleep yet?' His voice was mild, not that she had been expecting any of the animosity she knew he felt for her to show through—she didn't doubt that he still didn't feel very kindly towards her, but she was a guest who had been laid low, wasn't she? And the whole family seem to lay great stress on good manners.

'I ... I slept a lot at lunch time,' she offered by way of explanation for being wide awake.

'Have you had your tablets?' Dyson was looking down at her with a suggestion of a smile on the mouth she had always thought of as hard, but which surprised her by now having a softening curve to the bottom lip. She jerked her eyes away, wishing she could speed the growing agitation she was experiencing as quickly.

'I thought I wouldn't take any more.' And at his enquiring look, 'The pain isn't so bad now.'

Dyson didn't offer any comment to that, but studied her face, searching her eyes for any look of strain. And Amber's agitation grew as he pulled a chair forward and sat close to her. He was casually dressed in slacks and sweater and still loomed large even when seated.

'I'm sorry I have to stay in bed tomorrow,' Amber said in a rush. 'I ... I'll be up on Saturday, though.'

'We'll see.'

'Oh, I will,' she replied confidently. 'If only I hadn't been so stupid this morning ...'

'We both have something to regret about this morning,' Dyson told her, and she saw from his expression how bitterly he was regretting his actions. Knew he was aware she had ridden Bluebell when she had known it was too soon for that sort of adventure, purely in order to put as much distance between them as quickly as possible. The agitation she had been feeling since he had come into her room disappeared.

'Please don't—don't worry about it, Dyson,' she said impulsively. 'It doesn't matter ...'

'It does matter,' he said coldly. 'I had no right to treat you, a guest in my house, the way I did.'

'But you thought you had good reason,' she said, recalling that the remark she had flung at him in his study that morning must have sounded like an admission to all he believed, that taunt of 'What's the matter? Crabby because it wasn't you I welcomed?' She didn't like that dark look of self-recrimination on his face and hurried on unthinkingly, wanting only to dispel it. 'I let you believe that Simon and I had ...' She stopped, realising she had almost told him nothing had happened between her and his stepbrother. 'Oh,' she muttered, and looked away from him.

'Oh, indeed,' said Dyson. Then he shook her by saying, 'I know quite well that nothing happened between you and Simon last night—though if I know Simon, he didn't leave your room without chancing his arm first.'

'Er—you've seen Simon again?' She couldn't very well tell him Simon *had* 'chanced his arm', and to use Simon's expression, got the big E for his pains. But since Dyson now knew nothing had happened, and since everything she had said to him up to now was contrary to that, then Simon must have told him after all.

'I have seen Simon since our talk after lunch,' Dyson agreed, 'but we didn't discuss his nocturnal activities.'

Oh,' Amber said again, and felt an unexpected rush of pleasure that despite all the damning evidence of his own eyes in seeing Simon coming from her room in the early hours, Dyson no longer believed she and Simon had been lovers. She couldn't understand the happiness that came over her that because Dyson Silver, the man she had thought only that morning she hated, was giving her the benefit of the doubt. 'Nothing happened between us,' she confirmed, in direct opposition to her earlier thought that she wanted him to go on believing something had happened. And even though Dyson had asked for no explanation, she found herself telling him, 'My light was on when Simon came home—he saw it from beneath the door. He—he came in.'

It had been on the tip of her tongue to add that Simon had come in purely to see if she was all right, but the words wouldn't roll off her tongue—it seemed vital somehow that she was completely honest with Dyson now. And she was glad when Dyson didn't ask why Simon had thought it necessary to enter her room —he knew his brother better than she did.

'Tell me, Amber, do you usually sleep with the light on?'

'No—no.' She hadn't expected that question, and knew her monosyllabic answer was not going to be sufficient as a short silence followed that one small word. She knew Dyson was waiting for her to continue. 'I'd had a bad dream—and . . . and . . .'

'And were frightened to go back to sleep again?'

'Yes,' she admitted.

'You've had this same dream before?' Dyson probed gently, and Amber was amazed at the wealth of understanding coming from this man she had dubbed as being harder than granite.

'Not for a long time,' she confessed. 'I thought it had gone for good when the pain went.'

'You were in pain last night?' he asked, his eyes alert. He was too quick for her.

'No—not really.' And as his gaze fixed on her, she found it impossible to tell even the whitest of lies. 'I had ricked it earlier in the day—but it was ...'

'How did this happen?'

There was nothing for it, she thought, a feeling of unease creeping over her that Dyson was in no hurry to go, and if he wanted his question answering, he was the sort to sit there all night until she was ready to tell him.

'Oh—well, if you must know, Simon had made a grab for me under the mistletoe.' She looked away from the hard light that suddenly entered his eyes, and finished edgily, 'You appeared from nowhere and I know you thought I was thoroughly enjoying Simon's em—embrace, when in actual fact I was hanging on to him because I hadn't got my balance.'

Amber looked at Dyson again, and guessed from his look he would be having a few more words with Simon about his 'horse play', and knew Dyson was regretting he had been none too gentle with her himself. But she couldn't bear that she should be the cause of more trouble between the two brothers.

'It was my own fault,' she said. 'Simon didn't know about my accident—he'll be more careful in future.'

Dyson seemed to accept that, for he made no comment on it, but returned to asking her what her bad dream had been about. Not wanting to tell him, and hesitantly at first, Amber found herself talking out her nightmare. And it seemed the most natural thing in the world when she came towards the end to find Dyson had hold of her hand on the coverlet. 'They said both my parents were killed instantly—that they couldn't have suffered—but I always wake up at the point where my mother is calling for me to help her and I can't move because I'm half buried too,' Amber finished huskily.

Dyson heard her out to the end, then he raised the hand he was holding and brought it up to his lips. As if she had stepped out of a dream, Amber watched his action, felt his lips warm on the back of her hand, and then, still not believing it, the words penetrated her mind, 'I love him', and it didn't seem at that moment to be the earth-shattering discovery it was. She smiled at him and felt her hand returned to the coverlet, her eyes turning away from him to stare at her hand in wonder.

'So that's why you were still awake when I came in— because you're afraid to sleep in case your nightmare returns?' His voice sounded no different from the kind tone he had used earlier, but hearing his voice effectively brought Amber out of the trance she had found herself in.

'I'm not feeling very sleepy,' she replied.

Dyson stood up and she had the dreadful feeling he was going to go, so she kept her features immobile so he shouldn't know she wanted him to stay with her. Her relief was out of all proportion when he said conspiratorially, 'I'm not sleepy either—do you mind if I stay with you a while longer?'

Amber had no hesitation in saying, 'Would you?' knowing he would think it was purely because she didn't want to be on her own and risk falling asleep and having her nightmare return.

Dyson picked up her bottle of tablets from off the bedside table. 'I think a couple of these will help you,

Amber. Will you take a couple to please me?'

She would have done anything he asked just then; taking a couple of tablets was nothing compared to what she would do for him if asked. 'Yes,' she said, and waited while he went into the bathroom and came back with a glass of water.

'You don't appear to have many of these left,' he observed as he up-ended a couple of the tablets into the lid. 'When did you last see Dr Cresswell in his professional capacity?'

Amber had no trouble remembering. 'It was September, the day after ...' She stopped there, aware her tongue was running away with her.

It was nothing short of heaven to feel Dyson's arm behind her shoulders as he held her in steely support while she swallowed the tablets. But the contact was too short, and almost at once she was settled down in bed again with the glass she had used resting on the bedside table, Dyson once more seated on the chair near her.

She thought he had finished questioning her about her last professional visit from Uncle James, and a feeling of disquiet washed over her as he said in easy conversation:

'You were saying the last time you went to see Dr Cresswell was in September ...'

'He came to see me, actually,' said Amber, hoping to head him off.

'You were too ill to go to his surgery?'

She had a distinct conviction that people like Dyson were not so easily headed off once they had made their mind up to something.

'No, I wasn't ill.' Dyson was sitting there quietly, his very silence forcing her to go on. 'I ... I was upset.'

'Because you believed you had only six months to live?'

She had thought to hear a softer note in his voice at that, but if anything she could hear a hard note creeping in. It stiffened her own attitude—she hadn't yet got used to the knowledge that she had fallen in love with him, but instinct was at work telling her it wouldn't do for him to discover her feelings for him.

'Uncle James shouldn't have told you about that!'

'To be fair to him, he thought I already knew.'

Amber almost gasped at this until she recalled that Dyson had been in the room when Uncle James had been stressing the point that her condition wasn't terminal. She wondered what else Uncle James had told him—as her host Dyson had a right to know certain things about anything to do with getting her on her feet again. Though, she thought, there wasn't very much else for Dyson to know. Uncle James himself had never known the real reason for her wanting to see him that day, and she would take good care neither Uncle James nor Dyson ever did know about it either, she thought, with hardening resolve.

'You poor child,' Dyson said with such unexpected gentleness that her hardened resolve immediately took a header out of the window. 'Of course you were upset. Thank God you had enough courage to tell Dr Cresswell all that you'd overheard in that hospital—you must have been in torment!'

She wanted to say it hadn't been as bad as all that, for Dyson's sympathy was making her feel weepy. But it had been worse than bad; never again did she want to go through those panic-stricken days.

'Yes—well,' she said lamely, and began to feel relaxed again, as the threatening tears retreated, she was even beginning to think she felt a little sleepy. That was until Dyson asked quietly:

'You were saying you asked Dr Cresswell to call the day after ... The day after what, Amber?'

'Er——' It was no good, her powers of invention seemed to have deserted her, and nothing was coming through except the truth. She flicked a glance in Dyson's direction, but wasn't fooled by that encouraging look. He meant to be answered, and she had a distinct impression he would know the truth from a lie, had a distinct impression he knew full well it had been after that particular night too.

'You know anyway, so why make me tell you?' She knew any time now they would be back to being enemies.

'It was the day after you'd spent the night in bed with me, wasn't it?'

'Yes.'

'You *were* ill afterwards.'

Again the feeling came over her that she didn't want him to feel remorse about anything connected with her.

'I told you I didn't remember anything of what had happened,' she told him, her cheeks glowing crimson. 'I wasn't ill,' she repeated, and growing angry that he had the power to play ducks and drakes with her powers of rational thinking. 'I was just—just upset, that was all.'

'Dr Cresswell told me you were heartbroken when you told him you thought your time on earth was limited—I'm beginning to know you, Amber, and from what I know of you, I'm wondering, when you hadn't told him in all the time since you overheard what the consultant in hospital said, what triggered off your need to confide in him all of a sudden. Was it just that it all became too much for you? That I can understand, of course—dammit, you should have told him straight away, he could have saved you all you went through. But there's something in you, Amber, a privacy of person, that keeps you bottled up.'

Amber no longer wished for Dyson to stay with her. He was too sharp, too brilliantly assessing; he hadn't got where he was without being able to sift through the most complicated of issues and not be able to unravel its intricacies.

'What was it that upset you so much you had to tell him?' Dyson paused, waiting for her reply, then went on, 'You'd spent a night in my bed—you've already told me you can't remember anything that happened, but I'm convinced it was something that ...'

'Please stop!' It was a plea from her heart, but she saw from his narrow-eyed look that having once assured himself there was something even more terrifying to her than the knowledge she already had, Dyson wasn't going to heed her plea. Even if he didn't learn the answer here in this room, some time, even if it was after she had returned to Exeter, he was going to find the answer he was seeking—and she just couldn't bear that he should come and ask her for confirmation. Far better to get it said and finished with. He was being kind to her now because she was confined to her bed. But when she was well again, he would adopt the same cynical manner he had had before, and now that she knew she loved him, she didn't think she could bear it. When she left here—it would be better if she never saw him again.

'I mean to know, Amber,' he told her quietly, and she knew if she didn't tell him he would go and see Uncle James, might even tell him about that night.

'I thought I was pregnant.'

Her words fell into a hushed silence. She heard the hiss of Dyson's indrawn breath that told her belatedly his thoughts had not been running along those lines at all. She was almost beside herself because it was not fair, it just wasn't fair, that he had got that confession out of her when he would never have guessed anyway.

'Yes—pregnant,' she said furiously. 'You wouldn't have cared, would you? B-but I cared. I thought I'd conceived your child—knew the baby stood as little chance as I did of survival,' tears were falling like rain from her eyes, but she was too het up to notice. 'Can you have any idea what it feels like to be convinced you've conceived an innocent child and to know that that child will die with you—I wanted that baby,' her voice broke on a sob, her words fading. 'I wanted that baby to love!'

CHAPTER NINE

AMBER closed her eyes, rested her amber-lit head on her pillow, and thought—there, it was all out. She hadn't wanted to tell him, there had been no real need to tell him. He would never have guessed, and he was probably now adding a few more names to the string he already had for her. She wished he would go. She felt then that she never wanted to see him again. That her confession had knocked him sideways she had no doubt, for she had seen the disbelieving look in his eyes, the greyness in his face she had seen once before that day. She wished, though, that she could stop crying. She felt the bed go down under his weight, and knew he had recovered from the shock her words had given him, but she didn't want him anywhere near her and pushed blindly at the bulk she knew would be there, only she didn't want to open her eyes. She felt her hands caught in his grasp, caught and held.

'Oh, my dear, dear Amber,' he said, and his voice sounded so hoarse, so strangled somehow, as if he was striving for control, only she just couldn't look at him to know that he thought her a complete fool. 'You've visited hell, haven't you?'

And then she did open her eyes, as very gently, so as not to hurt her, Dyson pulled her into his arms and cradled her head into his shoulder. 'I shall never forgive myself for all you've been through,' he said against her ear. And that wasn't what she wanted, that he should take some of the guilt.

'It wasn't your fault,' she said, and as he pulled his head back to look at her she felt a rush of colour wash over her. 'Y-you know what I mean,' she added quickly, and felt better when she heard his light laugh.

'Yes, I think I do know what you mean,' he said, and there was none of the hateful sarcasm in his voice. Then his voice still quiet, his arms still holding her in that comforting hold, he said, 'Tell me how you came to be in that hotel in the first place.' And Amber thought then that somehow, she didn't know how, Dyson had discerned that it wasn't a usual haunt of hers. He seemed to know, she thought, that it wasn't her way to plaster make-up on her face and sit on a bar stool waiting to be picked up.

It didn't seem strange at that time, with the rest of the house in bed and asleep, to be here with Dyson's supporting arms around her, to be telling him of her meeting with Sally, her urgent need to know something of life. 'I kept thinking I was twenty-two and there was so much I hadn't done, so many things I hadn't experienced,' she told him, wondering if she could make him see how she had felt at that time.

Apparently he did understand, but her relief at his understanding was shortlived when he asked, 'Was it in your mind to go to bed with the first willing man you met?' She thought the hand at her back moved tautly as he waited for her answer, but she couldn't be sure.

'Oh no, I hadn't been thinking along those lines at all. Sally had suggested this pub crawl, and it was something I'd never done—I couldn't bear another night staying at home with only myself for company—I was going mad with my thoughts.' This time the hand on her back definitely moved, but only in order to pull her closer against him. 'Sally didn't turn up and I started to get panicky again, so I did something I've never done before—another first,' she added, 'and started speaking to you. I ... I didn't care very much for the turn the conversation took, but it was better than fighting the panic that was growing inside me. When you suggested having a drink in your room I knew what was going to happen—but I went with you. I was used to waking up in the middle of a nightmare— I think I was more concerned then with having the comfort of another human being with me when I woke up.'

'Did you have a nightmare that night?' Dyson asked, looking down into her face.

'No, I didn't,' Amber told him. 'I woke up, saw you in bed next to me and have never felt so ashamed in my life.'

'And then you began to think you were pregnant?'

'Oh, not then. That was after I got home. Sally rang and something she was talking about put the idea into my mind.'

'So you rang Dr Cresswell.'

'Yes—but before I could get round to telling him the real reason I was so upset, I told him what I'd overheard in hospital—and as soon as he had convinced me I'd made a mistake, there didn't seem any point in telling him about—the other—not for a while anyhow.'

'You planned to keep the baby?'

'Yes—I know it sounds ridiculous now, but I was actually looking forward to it.'

Dyson's arms became an iron bar around her as, asked by him how she planned to manage, she told him about giving in her notice at Turner, Turner & Scott, and about the money she would receive from her parents' estate.

'You're a very courageous young lady,' he said, when she came to the end.

Amber didn't think she had been very brave at all. But there was a look so tender in his eyes, as though he was suffering all that she had suffered, that in a moment of complete empathy she leaned forward and placed a kiss on the side of his face.

'Don't feel bad about your part in all this—you weren't to know,' she said gently.

Dyson's dark eyes fastened on her as though her kiss had been as much a jolt to him as anything else that had gone before. 'A very courageous young lady,' he repeated, and then he in turn kissed her, not on the cheek the way she had done, but on her slightly parted mouth.

Amber went hot and cold when she thought about it afterwards. It had been meant purely and simply as a kiss in empathy of the moment. Dyson hadn't expected her arms to go round him, that much she knew, but she couldn't seem to stop herself, and when his mouth left hers, she wanted him to kiss her again. His eyes met hers, and she knew he had read what she wanted.

'No, Amber,' he said, and there was emotion in his voice as he said it. 'I think we're both feeling vulnerable at the moment—this situation is too explosive.' He took his arms away from her, but Amber didn't move, and almost as if he couldn't stop himself, Dyson's arms came round her again. 'You're too much for me . . .' He didn't finish, but gave in to her, and Amber thought his kiss was the most wonderful thing she had ever known as gently at first, his mouth rested on hers, then as her lips parted invitingly, the pressure increased.

He was still supporting her strongly with one arm, but as she clung to him, he allowed one hand to caress her shoulder, to slip her wide-necked nightie down her arm. She felt the whisper of his kiss on her shoulder where his hand had been, then his lips were at her throat, trailing tender kisses into the hollows, across and up to her ear. Her body felt as though it was singing as she delighted in his touch. There was none of the ruthless passion there that had been there this morning.

Amber was unaware, in moving her arm to grip his waist, as taking care not to jar her, Dyson adjusted his position, that the ribbon tie of her nightdress that was sometimes troublesome, had come undone as one end caught between them. Then as Dyson's lips claimed hers once more and she became lost as his ardour increased, she wanted to put her arms round him again to hold him to her, but found she couldn't because her nightie had slipped down both arms and was holding her arms to her sides. His lips searched the pleasures hers had to hold for him. She felt the tip of his tongue tantalising her bottom lip, and in an instant, as her need for him mounted, she pulled her arms free, uncaring that her nightdress was working its way down to her waist, as she placed her naked arms around him and held him to her.

'Oh, Amber,' he muttered, his mouth leaving hers, and she thought from his tone he meant to put her away from him, but that wasn't what she wanted.

'Kiss me, Dyson,' she breathed against him, and saw the fire light up in his eyes that told her he found her desirable and irresistible. Then with a groan she didn't understand, his mouth was on hers again, and everything in her upbringing that said now was the time to stop was ignored, as she felt his gentle hands caressing her back.

Suddenly, as though it had just got through to him that the back of her was uncovered and it therefore followed that the front of her was too, Dyson pulled away from her, and she saw the fire in his eyes become an inferno. At his quickly indrawn breath, her eyes followed his, and she saw his look had settled on her uncovered breasts.

Scarlet colour flooded her cheeks. 'I didn't know,' she said, and grabbed to drag the folds of her nightie back to her, but didn't manage it because Dyson's hand stayed her.

'No,' he said, his voice low. 'You're beautiful,' and his hand came out and with a butterfly touch as if afraid he would harm her, his fingers caressed round the swollen contours of her, sending shivers of ecstasy along her spine, until at long last he touched the hardening pink tips, and it seemed to her then that she would not wake up in the morning alone in her bed. And she closed her eyes, because it was more than she could take—this feeling of joy without shame.

What had happened to Dyson in that moment when she closed her eyes, Amber didn't know, for enraptured with the anticipation of being his completely, she felt his hand leave her, and opened her eyes, not to see the man she loved as delirious with passion as she was, but a man who was struggling to damp down the fires that she knew were raging inside him.

'One of us has to be sane,' he said levelly, and if he was having trouble in keeping his voice level, she was unaware of it for all there was a dull flush of colour in his face. 'I'm afraid, much as your charms threaten to sink me, we must remember that any movement is painful to you.'

Damn the pain, Amber wanted to tell him, she hadn't felt a thing the whole time he had been loving her. But she saw Dyson had already withdrawn from her—to ask him to kiss her again, was just asking to have the door slammed in her face.

She couldn't look at him as he helped her back into her nightie, wouldn't look at him as he saw to it she was lying comfortably on her side and pulling the covers up around her.

'Try to sleep, Amber,' he said gently, and she knew

sleep was a million miles away, as he silently left her room.

She fell into a dreamless sleep shortly after he had gone, and woke early the next morning barely able to believe it as remembrance hit her of what had gone before he had left her in the solitude of the room. She groaned aloud and wished it was her own bed she had awakened in, wished that she was back in Exeter with the need to ever see him again past.

She didn't wonder at how she had come to love him when she had been sure she hated him. Dyson had been kind to her last night, had listened while she had told him practically everything there was to know about her. Hot colour washed over her as she recalled the way she had clung to him, had shown no shame when she had all but invited his intimate touch. If he had been beginning to revise his opinion of her and her lack of morals, she had given him full proof that basically she was still the hussy he had first thought.

She had no need to think about what his feelings towards her were; she had witnessed before a sensitivity in him that had surprised her. It had been that sensitivity that had been her undoing. She had thought he had understood and not found her wanting, but as soon as she had clung to him he had reacted in a way any red-blooded male would react. That he had desired her, wanted her as she had wanted him, didn't mean anything. Heaven help her, hadn't his basic masculine urge been in evidence that night last September? He had taken her then without knowing anything about her. There had been no love in that. And last night, when he had already told her when he had hauled her out of the bath that he had no personal interest in her, had it not been for fear of causing her pain, he could have taken her again—and he had known it.

Amber thought she would never be able to look him

in the face again. She was sure his manner when next she saw him would have returned to being cynical and jibing. Oh, if only she could go home! It had been arranged that she would drive into work with Helen on Monday morning—she had another three days to live through with every chance of being left alone with Dyson. Well, thank goodness she still had her pride. Not by word, look or deed was he going to know how she felt about him.

Gingerly she reached for her watch, and found the movement caused her no pain. Thank the lord for that, she had done herself no harm that a day in bed hadn't put right. She felt more guilty than ever. She could quite easily get up today, but at least if she stayed in bed, always supposing Dyson would let her get up, she would be out of his way. She didn't hold any illusions that he would come in tonight when everyone else was in bed to see if she was all right. She had shown him she was easy, there was no challenge in that, and challenge was the spice of life to Dyson Silver. She had no need to look further than the deal Simon said he had pulled off when all the odds were against him. She looked at her watch. Seven o'clock.

Having thought it would be another half an hour at least before Maureen brought up her early morning tea, Amber was startled to see her bedroom door being quietly opened. Her senses set up a chaotic clamouring when she saw Dyson checking to see if she was awake, then closing the door behind him and coming further into the room.

Instantly she veiled her eyes. Her first glance had noted that he was dressed much in the same way he had been last night, in slacks and sweater. She didn't know what he was doing in her room so early, but the thought that perhaps he had judged that her back would be better this morning and had come to take up what she had been so eagerly offering last night was strong enough for her to harden her heart against him.

'Good morning,' she said coolly before he could speak. 'To what do I owe this unexpected pleasure?' She had never thought herself capable of injecting such sneering ice into her voice, and couldn't help being proud of herself when she saw his face take on a tight-lipped look. Still not waiting for him to say anything, knowing his sarcasm would have the power to shrivel her up into a sick knot of hopelessness, she went on, 'If you've come early looking for a bargain, I'm afraid you're out of luck.' She was convinced suddenly that he had woken up in an amorous mood. 'No sale, Dyson,' she said coldly.

He didn't have to use words, though she could see from the thunderous expression on his brow that he hadn't taken kindly to the change in her; his killing look spoke volumes.

'Contrary to your highly esteemed opinion of me,' he said cuttingly, 'I have not come to barter for your services, which up to now I believe have always been for free.' Oh, he was cruel, his words cut into her like a knife edge. 'But as the medical profession get to work early in the day, I want to satisfy myself that you're capable of standing upright. Should that not be the case, I shall be able to summon medical help without having too much trouble.'

There was nothing in him now to remind her of the sensitivity she had thought he possessed. His tone was only just this side of being vitriolic, and she could see far from wanting to embrace her, kiss her, he looked as though he was having a hard time in keeping his hands from strangling her. He was right, of course, as ever, she thought sourly. Had he waited until a more reason-able hour to check on her, then it might be hours be-fore medical assistance could be brought to her, though she didn't thank him for his foresight.

'I'm better,' she said shortly. He could go hang himself before she would stand up for him!

'Right, then prove it.' Stubbornly Amber stayed where she was. She had no intention of getting out of bed while he was there. 'Do you want some help?' he asked insidiously.

She knew him well enough, she thought, to know that if she didn't make some move, he would come and hoist her out of bed. None too gently either, by the look of him—she wasn't worried about any pain he might cause her, but had an idea her iron will power against him would melt if he so much as touched her. Dyson took a step nearer. It was enough to have her going into action.

'Don't touch me,' she said quickly, and saw an exasperated look cross his face. She was sure his expression had been one of exasperation, she thought, as she pushed back the covers and pulled her feet over the side of the bed, though for a fleeting second she had thought she had caught a glimpse of the same sick feeling she was experiencing. Nonsense, of course. If Dyson was feeling sick at all, it was entirely because he had to put up with her being a guest in his house until next Monday.

'Stand up!' she was commanded.

Oh damn, that stupid tie of her nightdress had come undone during the night and the front of it was gaping open, the naked swell of her breasts, the shadowed valley between clearly on view. She couldn't help the glance she flicked at him. She saw his eyes had gone to the front of her, and looked hastily away, hurriedly retying the slippery nylon, as she saw his mouth form a tight line. Her dressing gown was hanging in the wardrobe, but she wasn't going to bring his attention to her embarrassment by asking him to get it for her, she would be back in bed as soon as she had proved to him that she could stand unaided. And anyway, he had seen far more of her since carrying her from the bathroom yesterday.

Knowing his patience was very thin this morning, she pulled herself upright. 'There,' she said, straightening her shoulders. 'Satisfied?'

Dyson didn't answer her. She thought he was going to leave her without another word, for he turned his back on her and began to walk away. But when he reached the dressing table he turned.

'Now let's see if you can walk.' His look was purely impersonal. 'Come here,' he said.

'Oh, really!' Amber objected, but she knew she had to comply, and was glad as she started towards him that she was standing straight, her hunchback stagger of yesterday a thing of the past. She grew confident with each step, as pleased with herself as if she had just discovered something new—it had passed through her mind in a weak moment yesterday to wonder if she would ever straighten up.

She stopped when she was about a yard or so away from him; she hadn't wanted to go that far but thought two or three steps wouldn't satisfy him. 'Can I go back to bed now?' she asked coolly, and without waiting for his answer, swung round—swung round too quickly and lost her balance. It happened so quickly, she thought she was going to disgrace herself and fall in a heap at his feet, but before that could happen she felt two strong arms come round her preventing her fall.

The instant Dyson touched her, her will power against him was as nothing, and it was instinctive to lean against him, to savour the hardness of his chest against her. But whatever he felt at that contact, it certainly wasn't the same effect she felt, for he pushed her away from him, his hands holding her steady.

'Not so clever as you thought you were, are you?'

'I ... I lost my balance in turning, that's all,' Amber fired back, recovering rapidly. 'If you could bring yourself to let go of my arms,' she snapped, striving for some of his sarcastic aggression, 'I'll get back to bed.'

'Get back, and stay there,' he said grimly, letting go of her.

She knew from that that doctor's orders were going to be obeyed to the letter that day. Dyson didn't hang about once she moved, he stayed only to see she was safely in bed, then went out without saying another word.

Amber found that like yesterday, once the household was astir, she was not left alone for very long. Though in the time between visits, and Helen was the most constant visitor, she had too much time to reflect on what had happened first thing that morning. She guessed that Uncle James had suggested to Dyson when they had been closeted in his study yesterday the need to see if she could walk this morning, but she could have wished Dyson had left it to Helen to report back to him, or even been prepared to take her own word for it. But it was too much to hope he would take her word for anything. Why, he was probably this morning discounting most of what she had told him last night anyway. There had been none of the tenderness he had shown when she had told him how she had come to be in that hotel—it had been all he could do to be civil to her. She decided there and then that the next time Helen came to see her, she would sound out the possibility of leaving before next Monday—she wasn't staying anywhere where the host thought she was lower than low, regardless of whether Dyson and Simon flared up at each other or not.

Helen came in armed with a stack of magazines. 'Dyson's just been out and bought these—should keep boredom away for a while,' she announced.

'Oh, thank you,' said Amber, not thinking Dyson had fetched them especially for her. 'I was wondering, actually, Helen,' she began, and found it dreadfully difficult to continue as everyone had been so kind to her, 'if you would mind if I went home tomorrow?'

'Amber, you can't!' Helen protested at once. Then slowly, seeing more than Amber had thought, 'Aren't you happy with us?'

'Oh, it isn't that,' Amber was quick to reply, feeling mean that she was repaying Helen's kindness this way. 'But—but ...'

'It's not because you think you're putting us to any trouble, is it?' Helen asked. 'You're not, Amber, honestly you're not. I'd feel simply terrible if you thought that.'

'I-I——' Amber faltered, knowing that to tell the truth, the truth that she didn't want to see Dyson again, would have Helen wanting to know why.

'Please stay, Amber,' Helen begged. 'Dyson and Simon have been on their best behaviour since you've been here and ...'

'All right,' Amber gave in, knowing she had put up only a puny fight in face of Helen's opposition. 'I've enjoyed my stay,' she said with more gratitude for Helen's kindness to her than with truth.

'Except for yesterday and today,' Helen smiled. 'Never mind, you'll be downstairs with us again tomorrow—you'll be glad to leave your bed.'

Of the two Amber thought if staying in bed meant she didn't have to see Dyson, then she would rather stay in bed. Though as the day wore on and she saw and heard nothing of him, she cancelled out that thought too. She wanted to see him, wanted to be in the same room with him, even if he couldn't bring himself to speak to her ever again.

Though he was outwardly courteous as befitted his role as her host, when Amber joined the others downstairs the next day, she was vividly aware that Dyson was keeping his distance with her. Any empathy that had been between them that night he had come to her room had long since gone. He was out a good deal of the day, so she was spared the need to keep up appearances. But he was there when the four of them sat down to dinner, and as Amber didn't feel she wanted to make any conversation that would bring his attention on her, she was glad that Helen and Simon were in fine form and kept up a flow of chit-chat that hid from them that she was saying very little.

Helen was saying how lovely and peaceful it would be when Simon returned to university, when Simon remembered his thesis and Amber's offer to type it.

'Did you mean it?' he asked. 'Would you really type it for me, Amber?'

'Of course I meant it.' It would be small return for the generous way she had been allowed to spend Christmas with them, besides which it would give her something to do in the evenings as well as enable her to brush up on her typing speeds. 'I have a typewriter at home . . .' she was saying, when Dyson's voice cut across her.

'I don't think it's a very good idea for Amber to do your typing, Simon,' he interrupted smoothly, and Amber's eyes flew to his hard gaze. He doesn't want me to have any contact with Simon once I leave here, she thought, the idea making her feel ill that he believed she might somehow corrupt his younger stepbrother.

'You don't?' Simon asked, and it was obvious Simon couldn't see any good reason why she shouldn't help him out.

Amber felt the heat come to her face. Surely Dyson

wasn't going to leave it like that, without explanation? Though if he did come out with the truth of his thoughts, she felt she would die to hear them voiced.

'I think I'm right in saying that Amber gave up her job as a secretary because her spine wasn't strong enough after her accident to sit at a typewriter for hours on end,' Dyson explained.

He looked at Amber; they both knew that wasn't the real reason she had left Turner, Turner & Scott, but she forced herself to return his hard look undaunted. If he told anyone what she had told him, that she didn't think old Mr Turner would view a prospective unmarried mother in a very kindly light, then Dyson himself, as the prospective father, wouldn't come out of it smelling exactly of roses, would he? She couldn't help the blush that stained her cheeks, but could have done without Simon drawing attention to it.

'I'd forgotten about Amber's back,' Simon said, turning his eyes in her direction. 'Why, you're blushing, Amber.' Then kindly, 'Don't be embarrassed because you're not strong enough to keep your promise.'

Really, they were making her feel like somebody on her last legs, when in a couple of months she would be as fit as any of them, Amber thought, her blush turning into the heat of anger.

'I'll get one of my secretaries to type it for you,' Dyson was offering, but Amber was no longer interested in the conversation. It was all so much eyewash anyway; she knew the real reason Dyson didn't want her to be in touch with Simon.

Her stars, she thought, must have been in the right ascendancy, for as she went to her room on Sunday night, she had not once been left alone with Dyson. If he had planned it that way himself it could not have worked out better. He had an early appointment in the morning, so her goodbyes to him had already been said. There had been an awkward moment when she had stood up with Helen to leave the room and Helen had brought Dyson's attention to her.

'You won't see Amber again if you're going off early,' she reminded him.

'Neither I shall,' Dyson had replied, and although he had courteously come over to where they were standing, he hadn't looked as though he was going to lose any sleep over that.

'I'll say goodbye now, then,' said Amber, not wanting to prolong what was already painful. She held out her hand, and thought for one dreadful moment Dyson was going to ignore it, then felt her hand seized in a firm grip. 'Thank you for having me,' she trotted out politely, and saw his eyes narrow, as though he could do without her conventional phrases, then she went scarlet as she realised what she had just said.

'The pleasure was all mine,' he said cruelly, and Amber didn't wait for any more. If she had upset him with her polite sentence, he had just about annihilated her with his. Regardless of what it looked like to Helen watching, she dragged her hand out of his grasp and walked hurriedly from the room.

The next morning Helen insisted on carrying her suitcase out to the car, much against Amber's wishes. 'Got to save the strain on your back,' she said, cheerfully brushing aside Amber's protests. 'I would have thought about it without Dyson reminding me.'

So Dyson had made a point of telling Helen to see that she didn't lift anything heavy. Amber wished she could have gained some comfort that he might be concerned about her, but when boiled down, didn't it come down to the fact that he knew Helen very well and wasn't risking, should she again rick her back, that Helen might out of the goodness of her heart insist she return to Moor View to be looked after?

She and Helen were soon in the thick of it when they entered Brewsters. As most of the temporary staff had left, and since things had not yet settled down at the factory, Amber and Helen finished at five that evening of the opinion that Mr McGilly had been a little premature in letting some of the staff go.

'I'll come to your car with you and get my case,' said Amber, when with a heartfelt sigh of relief they clanged the door of Brewsters shut behind them.

'I'll give you a lift,' Helen insisted, and Amber wondered if she could see Dyson's hand in this, for all Helen had given her a lift before today.

She was sure of it when Helen pulled up outside her home and would take no refusal when she said she would carry her case up to her room. Amber went to the door to wave her off, then went into the kitchen to make her tea, her mind busy. She choked back a sob; she loved Dyson so desperately, and he thought she was nothing but a little go-getter, free and easy with her favours, a little tramp with her eye to the main chance. And yet, she thought sadly, she had thought he had seen through to the person she really was. It just showed how wrong she had been. By his very action in telling Helen to carry her case he had shown he was taking no chances—he didn't want her in his house again.

CHAPTER TEN

AMBER'S spirits were at a low ebb when she caught the bus home from work the following evening. Helen had asked how she planned to spend this New Year's Eve, and suspecting if she told her the truth, that she had nothing planned other than perhaps to go to bed early and slam the door shut on the worst year of her life, that Helen would immediately invite her to Moor View, Amber told her she would be seeing the New Year in with James Cresswell.

'He was very understanding about my coming to you for Christmas,' she had added, and just in case Helen tried to overrule her, 'I think he might be hurt if I don't join him tonight.'

After changing out of the clothes she had worn that day, Amber set about making a meal she wasn't particularly interested in, and regretted the need to lie to Helen. She had been such a good friend, and she valued that friendship, but Helen must never know what had been between her and Dyson, and the lie had been necessary. Never again would she voluntarily put herself within a hundred yards of Dyson.

Clearing away the remains of her half eaten meal and attending to the washing up, Amber reflected she would have to do something about herself. Tomorrow was another year, for goodness' sake—that was something to look forward to. Who knew what the year held in store for her? She cheered up slightly at the thought that it couldn't be anywhere as bad as this one. Why, she might meet some dashing young man who would sweep her off her feet, a knight in shining armour who would come galloping up, want to marry her ... Her dream was shortlived; a hundred knights in shining armour couldn't oust the picture of Dyson that sprang immediately into her mind. Her lips twisted derisively. Even supposing she could forget she ever loved Dyson for long enough to agree to marry someone—who would want her when she confessed, as honesty said that she must, that she would be no bride in shimmering white, and why?

At nine o'clock Amber decided to go to bed. Her thoughts had been worrying at the same theme ever since she had got in. Dyson was the man she loved and she was prepared to believe she might get over that love given time, though just then it didn't seem that there would ever be a day when she wouldn't feel screwed up inside just thinking about him. But as for marrying anyone else, she couldn't think that would ever happen; she felt chained to him by that memory she didn't have, and didn't think any man could break that chain. She felt she belonged to him, but oh, how she wished she didn't!

She was on her feet ready to go upstairs when the front door bell sounded. She hadn't expected anyone to call, but a pleased smile curved her lips when she saw James Cresswell standing there.

'Hello, Uncle James, come in.'

'Thought you'd be living it up tonight,' he said, seeing she was in jeans and sweater. Amber forced a cheerful smile and took him into the sitting room, where he asked her how she was.

'Fine,' she said, and at his look, 'I am, honestly— that spot of trouble cleared up within twenty-four hours.'

'I thought it would—Why aren't you out celebrating, young lady? I was passing this way after making a call and expected to see the house in darkness.' Another twenty minutes and he would have done.

'I didn't feel like going anywhere tonight,' Amber explained, still trying to sound cheerful, though conscious of James Cresswell's close scrutiny of her.

'Why not come back and see the New Year in with me?' he suggested. 'I'm on call so I may have to go out, but Mrs Paget will be there.'

'I don't think so, Uncle James—I appreciate your asking, but . . .'

'But?'

Amber still showed him a cheerful face as she confessed, 'I'm not very good company tonight.'

'You're not in pain?'

'Oh no,' Amber replied quickly. 'No pain at all.'

James Cresswell didn't look entirely convinced. 'Have you any tablets you can take?'

'I don't need any.—I don't hurt anywhere.' Only this deep ache in my heart, she thought, and wished Uncle James could prescribe something to numb that pain as easily. She could see he didn't fully believe she wasn't still feeling a left-over twinge or two. 'I've got two tablets left if I need them,' she told him, so he should know she could do something about it if the pain returned.

'Only two? I'd better give you another prescription. What did I give you before?'

'You're an old fusspot,' Amber told him affectionately, and went to get the small bottle so he could refresh his memory.

'Hmm, these are strong,' he said as he studied the chemist's label. 'I'll give you something different, I think. I prescribed these when you were in severe pain—take more than two of these and you'll go out like a light.'

He was already busily scribbling on his prescription pad, and about to protest that she could buy

aspirin if she needed them, a cold shock passed over
Amber. 'Take more than two of these,' he had said,
referring to the bottle in his hand, 'and you'll go out
like a light.' He was handing her the completed prescription form before the whirl in her brain settled
down and she could ask him the all-important question she just had to have confirmed.

'You—er—you were joking about the strength of
these tablets, weren't you?' she asked, and swallowed
hard as she waited for his answer.

James Cresswell didn't see her expression because
he was returning his prescription pad to his doctor's
bag which he never left unattended in his car.

'Oh no—it's true,' he said, straightening up, his face
perfectly serious. 'Besides having a strong pain-killing
agent in them, there's also an additive that has a drowsing effect—take more than two and that drowsing
agent becomes a sleeping pill.' His voice became alert.
'You haven't had cause to take more than two at a
time, have you?'

'N-no.'

'That's good—though had that been the case you
wouldn't have felt pain or anything else for several
hours. Like I said, more than two of those and it would
be night-night, wake me in the morning.'

'Night-night, wake me in the morning,' Amber repeated when he had gone. She went back into the
sitting room and sank down heavily on the settee.
Suddenly, clearly, when all other memory had gone,
she could see herself in that bathroom of the hotel that
night—she had taken *four* tablets, she was sure she had.

Desperately she tried to think what had happened
after that, then her feelings became so agitated she
could no longer stay sitting down. What had she done
then—you'd think it would be imprinted for ever on
her mind? What was it she had done then? Yes, she'd

gone back into the bedroom, Dyson had given her a drink—she couldn't remember drinking any of it—but she'd had a drink downstairs in the bar, she could remember that clearly enough—it had tasted vile. She recalled now Uncle James jokingly telling her ages ago not to drink and drive. But she had drunk, and alcohol mixed with tablets ...

Convinced now she had flaked out on Dyson—hadn't lost her memory because she had been unconscious from the tablets and that glass of whisky, Amber felt her heartbeats set up a racing rhythm. She sat down, forcing herself to stay calm. What *had* happened after she had fallen into a drugged sleep? There was no way she was ever going to know, no way at all, not unless—not unless she asked the only person who could tell her.

Amber shrank away from the idea. She just couldn't ask Dyson—yet she had to know. The idea was growing and taking strength in her mind that she wasn't second-hand after all. She had got to know Dyson during that time she had spent in his house over Christmas, and though she still didn't know him very well, she knew he had a fine sensitivity to him, and though he had been as fed up as she had been that night—she had already worked out it must have been the same day he had discovered Simon had sold those shares—she was sure, positive with ninety-nine per cent of her mind, that he wouldn't have taken her in the state she was in. The one per cent doubt persisted. Had he been able to awaken her sufficiently to get some sort of response from her? She desperately had to know!

She shied from the idea of telephoning Moor View. What could she say? She couldn't very well say, 'Hello, Dyson—I'm just ringing to ask if you made love to me that night,' could she? Yet she would never settle until she knew.

Helen had written her number down in case she wanted to ring at any time, and feverishly now Amber sorted in her bag until she came across the slip of paper. Then, hardly knowing she was doing it, her fingers dialled the number. It seemed to ring out for an age, but she wouldn't put the phone down, just the brr-brr sound made her feel she was communicating with someone and helped to lessen the agitation she was feeling, though when at last she heard Helen's voice, she couldn't think of a thing to say.

'Hello,' said Helen for the second time, and afraid Helen would put the phone down before she could say a thing, Amber struggled to find her voice.

'H-Hello, Helen—it's me, Amber.'

Helen's voice changed to being welcoming. 'Hello, Amber,' then detecting something was not quite right with Amber's voice, 'Anything wrong? Are you calling from Dr Cresswell's home?'

'Er—no.' Helen's reminder that she had lied to her didn't help her to feel any better. 'Uncle James is on call tonight, so I didn't go after all.'

'Something is wrong, Amber ...' Helen began.

'No—n-nothing's wrong—er ...' What on earth did she say now?

Helen seemed to accept her statement at last. 'If you're sure ... Had you been ringing long? Simon's got a crowd of friends in and it's bedlam here.'

Amber couldn't see Dyson taking part in any of what he would term Simon's horseplay. Of course, he would be out, probably out celebrating with some sophisticated female—the thought was a knife thrust to her, but she squashed the searing jealousy that hit her, knowing Helen was hanging on to hear why she had called. It was less than five hours since she had seen her, so Helen would think it odd if she couldn't come up with some good reason.

Certain now that Dyson would be out, Amber said, 'Actually, I rather wanted a word with Dyson.'

'Oh,' Helen's tone was mildly curious, then she shattered Amber completely by saying, 'He's in his study, I'll put you through to his extension.'

'No!' The word was out sharper than she had intended as panic at what she had to ask him took over. 'No—it's all right, Helen,' she said more evenly. 'I don't want to disturb him—I . . . I'll call another time,' aware the even note hadn't lasted long. Then in case Helen would scoff and say, 'Talk to him now,' Amber said quickly, 'I shouldn't have rung on New Year's Eve. Happy New Year, Helen,' and without waiting for Helen to reply, she said, 'See you at the office the day after tomorrow.' She put the phone down, glad that New Year's Day was a Bank Holiday and that she wouldn't have to face Helen in the morning. She hoped by Thursday Helen would have forgiven her for terminating the call so abruptly.

Well, that was it, she decided nearly an hour later. Her impulse to ring Dyson and ask him to tell her what had happened had fizzled out. If only she'd had the courage to speak to him then, she would now be in possession of everything, good or bad, that she wanted to know. She still wanted to know—had to know, but could never see herself having the courage to ring and ask him, and to go to Moor View and ask him personally, to see his eyes harden cynically as she asked her question, she knew was completely beyond her.

Lost in her thoughts, Amber jumped, startled, when the front door bell went. Uncle James? Sure it was him on his way back from another call and probably popping in because he could see her downstairs light still on, she went to the door, composing her features into a smile. She pulled the door open, and searing hot colour washed over her face as her smile faded.

'Helen said you wanted a word.' Dyson stood there, his face unsmiling, looking totally in command, big and solid in his sheepskin jacket.

'You haven't come all this way . . . I . . . it could have waited.'

'Helen said you sounded upset.'

Conscious that it was a bitterly cold night and that she was keeping him standing on the doorstep, Amber said, 'You'd better come in.' She wished she'd had the courage to ask him over the phone. Dyson had a determined look on his face, and he hadn't driven thirty miles just to be told she had nothing specially she wanted to talk to him about.

She took him into the sitting room, and saw his glance take in that it was neat, tidy and comfortable. 'D-do sit down,' she invited, striving to remember her manners, her voice sounding high and unnatural.

'Have you anything to drink?' Dyson surprised her by asking.

'I'm sorry, I should have offered,' she said, knowing she wasn't coping very well. 'I'm afraid there's only sherry.'

'It isn't for me. By the sound of you, you need something to put you on an even keel.'

'Oh.' Amber strove to hide her agitation. This man saw too much—but she was glad to note he wasn't sounding sarcastic. 'I don't want a drink,' she said, and saw when she had sat down because her legs were feeling decidedly shaky that he had followed suit.

Dyson whom she had never thought to see again was here in her home, and she loved him with all her heart. She knew he didn't think very much of her and she was going to have to watch the distaste come over his face, as she knew it would, when she asked him to cast his mind back to that night last September. A disquieting thought came to her—What if he had forgotten what had taken place? A spasm of jealousy hit her again, but she forced her mind to think of it. Dyson was a virile man, and although he had remembered her face straight away, there must have been other girls in the last four months.

'I ... Dyson ... I ...' Oh, why couldn't she just spit it out—it would only take two minutes, then he would be gone.

Dyson moved, left the chair he had been sitting in and came unexpectedly over to where she sat on the settee. It did nothing for her agitated feelings when he sat down beside her and took her fidgeting fingers in his cool hold.

'You are in a state, aren't you,' he observed mildly. 'What's troubling you, Amber?'

'Dyson,' she began, wanting to wrench her fingers away but was finding he was holding her hand securely. 'Dyson—that night—you know the one I mean—the night we met ...'

'Yes?' His voice sounded encouraging, almost as if he wanted to help her over this bad moment, almost as if he knew what was coming—but he couldn't know, could he? Of course not—but ...

'Dyson, Uncle James popped in to see me tonight.'

'You're still having trouble?' he asked before she could continue, and she would have sworn at any other time his voice sounded concerned, but it was only her overwrought senses, she knew that.

'Oh no—he just happened to be passing.' She took a deep breath. 'Anyway, we got round to t-talking about my tablets—the ones he prescribed for me when I came out of hospital. Anyway,' she said again, realising she had already gone off the track of discussing that night in September, then thought that perhaps this was a better route. 'Uncle James told me that those tablets were very strong.'

'Yes,' Dyson said again, as if it was no surprise to him.

'Well—he ... he said as well as being strong pain-killers, they also had a—a strong drowsing agent in them, th-that if I took more than two I wouldn't know anything until I woke up.'

'I see.' She thought he was being remarkably patient in waiting for her to get to the point.

'Th-that night—the night we met ...' she paused, looked at him when it seemed he had nothing to say, and saw he was looking at her quite calmly, though there was a sharp look in his eyes. She bit her lip, not knowing if she was going to get to the end or not. She wanted to get up and walk around, but Dyson still had hold of her hand.

'Go on,' he said quietly.

Amber took a deep breath. 'That night,' she said, willing herself to stay as calm as he looked, 'when we got to your room—I went to the bathroom and took—*four* tablets.' There, she'd come to the end. Surely there was no need for her to go any further.

'So?' Dyson asked.

And the agitation, the agony of not knowing, of wanting to know, and having him calmly sitting there as if he didn't know what she was asking, found release in a small explosion of anger.

'So,' she snapped, snatching her hand away from him, 'if I flaked out like Uncle James had said I would do—You just tell me, Dyson Silver, what did happen?'

She saw his eyes narrow at her tone, and her spurt of temper died as suddenly as it had come. No one ordered Dyson to tell them anything. 'Please tell me,' she said huskily. 'I have to know.'

'Do you honestly think, Amber Newman,' he said, and she knew from the way he spoke she had touched a nerve, 'that I'm the sort of man who would find any pleasure in bedding an unconscious girl?'

'You didn't.' It was more a statement than a question, but there was no time to feel any emotion as she saw she had angered him by thinking such a thing of him.

'No, I didn't,' he stated clearly. 'And you can thank your stars for that. When I think you could have picked on just anybody that night, I go cold all over!'

'I'm sorry.' She wasn't quite sure why she was apologising, for it didn't seem to be doing his temper very much good.

'You're sorry! You damn well would have been had you picked on any of the bar-flies I saw there. What the *hell* do you think I am that you think I would take you, the state you were in?'

His anger was spurring on some heat of her own now. 'You weren't to know I'd taken too many pills,' she said hotly. 'You were as fed up as I was. How am I supposed to know how a man acts in a situation like that—you could have thought I was drunk.'

'As a matter of fact I did. But unconscious through drink or medication, you still didn't appeal to me.'

'Not much I didn't—you couldn't get me to that room fast enough!' Amber retorted, stung that he was making it obvious her charms were not of the holding sort.

Dyson flicked her a look as though to say he was tired of arguing with her. 'Had you been as sober up in that room as you appeared downstairs, I've no doubt I would have forced myself,' he told her with what she took for disgust in his voice, 'but when you swayed towards me and I got a face-full of whisky fumes, it put me right off.'

'Yet you still had me in your bed.'

'I put you to bed,' he corrected her, and she blushed that in the heat of the moment she had picked on the wrong choice of words. 'I took your dress off thinking you might care if it was creased when you came to, and apart from removing your shoes, I didn't touch you.'

So now she knew. She wasn't all those names she had been calling herself. She had known really, she supposed, ever since Uncle James had explained the strength of those tablets, had known that Dyson hadn't touched her. But all those months of having it fidgeting around in her mind, of feeling unclean whenever she thought of it, those thoughts, mingling with how cheap she must have appeared to him, seemed to bring about a great feeling of anti-climax. She felt the tears sting the backs of her eyes, and stared at her hands in her lap, unable to look at him any longer.

'I never—when Uncle James said about the tablets— I ... I couldn't think you'd ... I was sure you hadn't ...' she faltered, her voice thick with tears she wasn't going to shed. 'But I had to know for sure. I'm sorry if I offended you, Dyson—but I had to know for sure.' She hoped he couldn't see she was fighting for control, and after another few deep breaths, she said more clearly, 'I wish you'd told me before.'

'You almost begged me not to.' His voice sounded stiff and unyielding to the side of her, and she recalled the moment.

'Yes—but ...' Suddenly delayed reaction smote her at what he had allowed her to believe. It came to her then that he had been most unjust in not telling her. 'But you must have know why—you must have known it was because I thought I'd—we'd ...'

'Yes, I knew.'

His voice had been quite calm as he confirmed that he had known all along precisely what she hadn't wanted to know, and at his calmness Amber felt she wanted to hit him—to punch, to kick, to scream and yell at him, then she looked at him, and something in his expression, she didn't know what, but something there seemed to tell her he would almost welcome her violent retribution. Then before she could make any sense of her thoughts, he was saying:

'I should have told you—I wanted to many times—but ...'

'But thought it great sport to have me hating myself.' Amber interrupted dully, then, her anger getting the better of her, 'You must have been laughing yourself silly!'

'Laughing myself silly?' Dyson echoed harshly. The laugh's on me if anybody.' Amber went to interrupt him. 'Shut up,' he said grimly. 'I've said I wanted to tell you and I did. I knew it would mean a lot to you to know that nothing happened between us that night—to know that you'd left that room as untouched as you came into it—but for my own selfish reasons, I decided to keep the information to myself.'

Amber had not the vaguest idea why he should want to tell her and not do so. Selfish reasons, he had said; what possible selfish reasons could he have?

'Would it be too much for me to expect you to divulge what your "selfish reasons" are?'

She hadn't thought she had such sarcasm in her, and certainly not in the face of the dark look Dyson was favouring her with. She regretted her sarcasm the instant his hands came down on her shoulders in a hard grip. He hadn't liked her sarcasm, she could see that much, but when he spoke, his words, instead of breaking her into small pieces as she had expected, had her looking at him in wide-eyed disbelief.

'This is where you get to have the last laugh,' he said, and there was something in his voice that had her attention riveted on him. 'I didn't tell you about that night, because—because I went and did something that should give you quite a few moments of amusement whenever you think of it.—I, Amber Newman,' he said tersely, 'fell in love with you.'

'Fell in love with me?' She hadn't heard him right—couldn't have done. 'You just said . . .'

'I've just said I fell in love with you—Yes, I can see you don't believe it. I didn't believe it myself—but there had to be a reason why I should feel suddenly like murdering my own stepbrother when I saw him holding you at the bottom of the stairs.' Dyson took his hands away from her, turning his face away and staring blankly in front of him.

Amber couldn't doubt the sincerity of his words, yet it was too unbelievable to be true. 'You were jealous of Simon?' she asked, purely to gain time to let it sink in that Dyson was saying he loved her, that it wasn't a joke. There was nothing remotely jocular about his expression as she looked at him; he looked, she thought, for the first time since she had known him, defeated.

'Jealousy is a mild word for what I felt when I saw him coming from your room in the early hours of the morning—I spent the rest of the night in torment, and consequently put you through hell when we went into my study. I must have frightened the life out of you! I could see you were petrified, but thoughts of you and Simon were goading me on—I was almost insane with jealousy.'

'Oh, Dyson,' Amber whispered, in no doubt now what he was telling her was true. 'I'm so sorry.' She meant sorry that he had felt such a terrible emotion, a jealousy she too had felt, but had had no concrete evidence to feed it. It was clear when Dyson spoke again that he thought she was saying she was sorry that he had fallen in love with her.

'You have no need to be sorry, Amber,' he said quietly. 'I don't deserve that you should ever love me. After the way I behaved it's only fitting that you should hate me—though I had hoped it might be different.'

'Hoped ... ?' Amber said softly, when she wanted to fling her arms around him and tell him she could never hate him.

'Yes—hoped. That night when you told me of all the hell you've been through—about thinking you were pregnant ...' he paused, his face showing a fine sensitivity that her pain was his pain. 'I held you in my arms to comfort you—things got out of hand, but I didn't care—it was sheer delight to hold you in my arms, to feel you respond to me. I badly wanted you, Amber, but couldn't add to the pain you were in. I barely slept that night, thinking, hoping, hoping that in some small way you returned the love I have for you. I couldn't wait to come into your room the next morning to see if everything was still the same.' His face clouded over. 'When it came round to seven o'clock I couldn't wait any longer. I came to your room intending to just put my head inside your door— if you were asleep I would have gone out again. But you were awake, and left me in no doubt about your feelings for me. You showed me clearly that what had happened the night before was just a result of your highly emotional state, your need at that time for someone to hang on to—I've never felt so empty in my life.'

'Oh, Dyson,' Amber whispered huskily, the words she wanted to say to him locked in her throat as tears poured down her cheeks that in order that she might feel her honour satisfied, Dyson was casting his pride aside and baring his very soul to her.

He turned, his stern face taking on a gentle look as he witnessed her tears. He stretched out his hand, his forefinger smoothing a tear away from her cheek.

'You're so soft-hearted, my dear,' he said softly. 'I didn't mean to make you cry—I'd better go.' He made to get up, but Amber took hold of his hand and held it tightly.

'Please stay, Dyson.'

'No.' His reply was unequivocal. 'I must go while I have the strength to do so—I badly want to hold you in my arms, and you, I think, are tender-hearted enough to let me. Perhaps you don't hate me as much as I deserve, Amber—but if I hold you in my arms, my strength will desert me, I shan't be able to let you go—and tomorrow you *would* hate me.'

'I could never h-hate you, Dyson.'

A humourless smile touched his lips. 'You would, my dear.'

'I don't want you to go.'

Firmly he released his hand from hers. 'This is pure torture,' he said, standing up, 'and much though I deserve it—I can't take it.' He was at the door when Amber's voice halted him.

'I love you, Dyson.'

She saw his back go rigid. Then slowly he turned, his look as disbelieving as hers had been. 'You—love me?' he questioned, and his face was unsmiling, as though wanting to believe her but doubting whether her soft heart wasn't getting the better of her.

'I have done ever since that night you came to my room—you kissed my hand, and I knew then—I don't know how,' she said, feeling shy suddenly. 'I just knew I was in love with you. I thought—the next morning—

that your opinion of me had gone back to what it had been—thought you believed I was easy. I couldn't let you know I'd fallen in love with you.'

A tense moment followed her confession, and she watched as a convulsive movement passed over his face. Then the next instant he was beside her, she was in his arms and his mouth was coming down to plant exultant kisses over her face. 'Oh, my dearest girl,' he breathed, and then his lips claimed her as though he was starved for the touch of her.

When at last his lips broke from hers it was so that he could pull back and look into her eyes, his own alive with the love he had for her. 'It's incredible that you can love me after the swine I've been to you. When I think of it!' His arms tightened around her, then he held her away, his face unsmiling. 'You'll marry me?' he asked, as if there was some doubt about her answer.

'Please,' she said, and found her lips claimed again, his arms holding her tightly to him as though he would never let her go, as he took her on an upward spiral with his lovemaking. Her face was flushed, her hair disordered when he finally pulled away from her, and she saw the deepened colour about him too.

'I thought if ever I took you in my arms again, then nothing would stop me from making you mine,' he said, the huskiness in his voice telling her how much her unrestrained response had affected him. 'But all of a sudden I find myself being noble—I want you for my virgin bride.'

'Oh, Dyson!' Amber was deeply shaken that he had drawn back just when it had seemed he would possess her completely. She could see from the way his jaw was firmed that it hadn't been easy for him. She wondered at his self-control, and wanted to be his virgin bride, then she remembered—it seemed a long time ago now

—that she had told him blatantly she had had other lovers since him.

'There hasn't b-been anyone else,' she said quickly. 'I ... I mean, you will be the f-first ... I ...'

'I know, darling,' he cut her off.

'You know? But I told you there'd been ...'

'Been other men since that night in September?' His look was very slightly superior she thought when he said, 'Yes, I know you did—— You also told me, if my memory serves me right, that you had experienced none of the pain a chaste young female would feel at being ...'

'Oh!' Amber remembered him asking that question and her determination not to be caught out. A hot blush stole across her cheeks. 'I wasn't too bright, was I?'

'No, my darling, you weren't, and I thank you for it. I'd already started to have my doubts about you. The girl who looked desperate to get to church on Christmas Eve didn't quite tie up with the opinion I'd formed about you. Then like a lamb you were telling me, without knowing it, that you'd never been to bed with anyone—least of all Simon.'

Amber recalled that Dyson had told her he knew nothing had happened between her and Simon, without either of them telling him. 'So that's how you knew?'

Dyson leaned towards her and kissed her tenderly. 'That's how I knew, sweetheart.'

It was heaven to be held like this. Safe in his arms, secure in the unbelievable knowledge that he loved her, and for a while she was content just to sit in the shelter of his arms, then it came to her that he still hadn't explained everything.

'Why didn't you tell me about—that night, Dyson?' She was a little unsure of bringing the matter up, not wanting to disturb any of the blissful harmony between them, but since the thought had reared its head she was certain there must be some explanation. Dyson had known for some days that she wasn't the tramp he had first thought—she couldn't see why he should have kept it from her.

'It doesn't put me in a very good light, I'm afraid,' he confessed after a considering moment, and his arms tightened about her again as though seeking her understanding. 'But when I discovered the real you, discovered I loved you, wanted you to love me in return, I realised I'd done nothing to earn your love or even liking.' He was wrong there, but she didn't stop him, though the memory of how he had looked after her when she had hurt her back when riding Bluebell was very clear. 'I knew you weren't the promiscuous sort, knew, I thought, something of how you must be feeling about that night you didn't want to remember, and I thought feeling the way you did about it, you might in some way feel you weren't prepared to rush into another man's arms. I wanted you to feel you were committed to me. I was ready to start to woo you, was all prepared to stop by tomorrow—as though casually,' he confessed, 'to see if you would have dinner with me, and then I was going to begin a campaign of . . .'

'You were going to call tomorrow? If I hadn't telephoned tonight you would have called tomorrow anyway?'

'Oh yes—I had everything planned. I was going to be the model of patience, hoped you would begin to see me differently.'

'Dyson,' Amber breathed his name as an endearment, swinging from being disturbed at the information he had kept from her, to delight that he had wanted her to feel committed to him. She already was, and would be forever more.

'When Helen said you sounded upset on the phone, all my plans for a slow courtship took a flying leap. I couldn't get to you fast enough, and I knew as soon as I found out what was troubling you that all my plans, hopes, were doomed to failure. I couldn't do anything other than tell you the truth—tell you everything. God knows what I would be doing now if you had let me go out of that door.' His face looked bleak as he remembered.

'I love you, Dyson,' Amber said quietly, and was amazed that those few words should have the effect of altering his expression so rapidly. For instantly the bleak look left his face, and the eyes that stared into hers gave back an answering look of love. Nearby church bells could be heard ringing out. And Dyson's eyes left hers briefly to glance at the clock on the mantelpiece—the hands that showed midnight.

'Next year is going to be the happiest one of my life,' he declared, his eyes warm with love for her. 'And we'll have many more years of happiness together, my darling.' His kiss was tender, loving. 'Happy New Year, my dearest Amber.'

'Happy New Year, my dear, dear Dyson,' Amber said huskily.

Harlequin Plus

A GREAT ROMANCE AUTHOR

Amber's Christmas present from Dyson in *Intimate Enemies* is an expensively bound volume of *Jane Eyre*, a nineteenth-century novel by Charlotte Brontë. Many people consider this book to be the forerunner of the modern Harlequin romances.

Charlotte Brontë was born in Yorkshire, England, in 1816, one of six children. She grew up in a lonely village called Haworth, on the Yorkshire moors, where her father was a minister. When Charlotte was eight, she and her sisters were sent to boarding school, which was so badly run that two of them became ill and died. Charlotte was removed from the school, but the tragedy was to leave a deep impression on her. Charlotte used her memories to write about Jane Eyre's terrible experiences as an orphan at a school called Lowood.

Charlotte remained at home in the country with her surviving brother and sisters—Emily and Anne—for the next five years. To entertain themselves, the children invented the Kingdom of Angria and wrote in little notebooks about its rulers and battles and great love affairs. This simple children's game was the beginning of Charlotte's creativity.

As a young woman, Charlotte worked for brief periods as a teacher and governess—just like the character Jane Eyre. In 1846 Charlotte began to write *Jane Eyre*, which was published in 1847. It was an immediate success, and Charlotte, now famous, traveled to London to meet the great writers of her time.

In 1854, Charlotte Brontë married an Irishman, Arthur Bell Nicholls. She died tragically less than a year later, in 1855, of complications associated with her pregnancy.

Generations of women have enjoyed *Jane Eyre* for its threefold theme of love, independence and forgiveness; and Charlotte Brontë's heroine, Jane, has proved to be one of the most enduring and beloved characters in English literature!

Great old favorites...
Harlequin Classic Library

The **HARLEQUIN CLASSIC LIBRARY**
is offering some of the best in romance fiction—
great old classics from our early publishing lists.
Complete and mail this coupon today!

FREE BONUS BOOK

Harlequin Reader Service

In U.S.A. 1440 South Priest Drive
Tempe, AZ 85281

In Canada 649 Ontario Street
Stratford, Ontario N5A 6W2

Please send me the following novels from the Harlequin Classic Library. I am
enclosing my check or money order for $1.50 for each novel ordered, plus 75¢
to cover postage and handling. If I order all nine titles at one time, I will receive
a FREE book, *Doctor Bill*, by Lucy Agnes Hancock.

☐ 109 **Moon over the Alps**
    Essie Summers

☐ 110 **Until We Met**
    Anne Weale

☐ 111 **Once You Have Found Him**
    Esther Wyndham

☐ 112 **The Third in the House**
    Joyce Dingwell

☐ 113 **At the Villa Massina**
    Celine Conway

☐ 114 **Child Friday**
    Sara Seale

☐ 115 **No Silver Spoon**
    Jane Arbor

☐ 116 **Sugar Island**
    Jean S. MacLeod

☐ 117 **Ship's Doctor**
    Kate Starr

Number of novels checked @ $1.50 each =	$ _____
N.Y. and Ariz. residents add appropriate sales tax	$ _____
Postage and handling	$ _____ .75
TOTAL $	_____

I enclose _____
(Please send check or money order. We cannot be responsible for cash sent
through the mail.)

Prices subject to change without notice.

Name _____
(Please Print)

Address _____
(Apt. no.)

City _____

State/Prov. _____ Zip/Postal Code _____

Offer expires December 31, 1983.   30656000000